LIFE SHOULD BE SIMPLE FOR CLUNIE FINN. HER dreams go no further than hoping that spring will come, waiting for the daisies to bloom, watching for the ducklings that will swim behind their mother on the pond. But Clunie's world is wider than springtime, and there are people in it other than her loving father, her patient teacher, and her kind friend Braddy Macon. There are bullies who chase her after school; there are kids who chant, *"Clunie Finn, Clunie Finn, lock her up in a loony bin;"* and there is Leo Bannon, who will take any opportunity to taunt and harass her . . . for Clunie is retarded.

As Leo's harassment grows more sinister, Braddy Macon offers Clunie his protection and support—even when it will cost him his own popularity at school, and his girlfriend, the beautiful Sally Rowe. But Braddy cannot protect Clunie from the world, from cruelty and ignorance—from Leo Bannon.

Writing with the power and compassion that characterized his highly-acclaimed A *Day No Pigs Would Die*, Robert Newton Peck tells a stirring story that is as tender as it is horrifying. With bold strokes he creates a powerful human drama in which goodness and evil are acted out around an innocent victim.

Books by Robert Newton Peck

A Day No Pigs Would Die
Path of Hunters
Millie's Boy
Soup
Fawn
Wild Cat
Bee Tree (poems)
Soup and Me
Hamilton
Hang for Treason
Rabbits and Redcoats
King of Kazoo (a musical)
Trig
Last Sunday
The King's Iron
Patooie
Soup for President
Eagle Fur
Trig Sees Red
Basket Case
Hub
Mr. Little
Clunie

Clunie

ROBERT NEWTON PECK

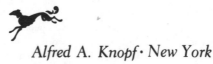

Alfred A. Knopf · New York

This is a Borzoi Book
Published by Alfred A. Knopf, Inc.

Copyright © 1979 by Robert Newton Peck
All rights reserved under International and Pan-American
Copyright Conventions. Published in the United States by
Alfred A. Knopf, Inc., New York, and simultaneously in
Canada by Random House of Canada Limited, Toronto.
Distributed by Random House, Inc., New York.
Manufactured in the United States of America

0 9 8 7 6 5 4 3 2 1

Jacket painting by Patricia Henderson Lincoln

Library of Congress Cataloging in Publication Data
Peck, Robert Newton. Clunie.
Summary: A teenage boy risks his own popularity to
give friendship and support to a retarded girl who is
harassed by her classmates.   [1. 'Friendship—Fiction.
2. Mentally handicapped—Fiction]   I. Title.
PZ7-P.339Cl. 1979 [Fic]   78-24335
ISBN 0-394-84166-2 ISBN 0-394-94166-7 lib. bdg.

Professor Wilbur Dorsett of Rollins College
inspired this story.

But I dedicate this book to kids
who can never read it, hoping that the
kids who can will care.

Robert Newton Peck

I

"HANG ON TIGHT, BOYS."

"You bet, Coach."

"Riding a skidder can be funny dangerous unless you brace your feet on the front plank, and take a firm purchase on the bracket. Lean back, so's you don't roll off. But if you *have* to tumble, make sure it's to the rear, *behind* the skidder."

Coach Hackman started the Ford.

"Here we go," said Wick.

Braddy Macon firmed his fingers around the bracket, watching Wicker Smith do likewise on his side. April had at last arrived, bringing enough sunlight to dry the March mud on the baseball diamond behind their high school. Time was ripe to drag the footprints and frost heaves off the diamond for outdoor practice. Slowly, the Ford lurched forward as Coach's left foot let out an easy clutch. Even so, both cables snapped taut, jerking the heavy wooden skidder.

"Ain't it fun?" Wick hollered.

Looking over his shoulder, Braddy Macon saw the smooth path that the skidder dragged across the reddy-tan loam of the infield. Around they went; whooping each time the skidder rumbled up and over the pitcher's mound, feeling the unyielding hardness of wooden planks beneath them. The dust on the skidder would smudge up the seat of his pants, and Wick's, but fun like this was too rich to miss.

"Hot damn!" yelled Wicker Smith.

Braddy knew that Coach Hackman wasn't driving his Ford very fast; but when he made a turn at home to follow the edge of the grass down the first-base line, the breeze blew his hair. The exhaust from the Ford even smelled near to tolerable. Spring was here.

"Real sport, eh, Braddy?"

Braddy Macon nodded. "Nifty."

Faces blew by them in the dust. Other students from Central High had come by to watch Coach drag the infield, and to see two members of the baseball team ride the skidder. Braddy felt proud that Coach had given him and Wicker Smith the honor. Even happier that Bannon wasn't around to hog it all for himself. Leo Bannon, the team captain, with his picture up on the wall in school. Red hair, muscles, and sly tricks to play on everybody. Always coming up behind you and jumping on your back.

Braddy had wanted Wick Smith for team captain; but instead, the redheaded catcher had won by a single vote. Braddy Macon shrugged to himself. I can live with it, he thought. Leo Bannon would make as good a captain as Wick; besides, Coach flashes the signals from the bench. All that Leo has to offer is a lot of mouth coupled with a hunger to win like he was starving to whip somebody. Yet he can catch.

"Practice tomorrow," said Wick. "I can't wait."

Braddy yelled back. "Same here."

A kid was shouting at him from the edge of the infield grass. "Hey, Braddy! Tell old Wick not to strain his pitchin' arm."

Without braking, as far as Bradford Macon could notice, Coach let his black Ford roll to a dead stop just as the skidder parked itself behind the bleachers.

"My butt hurts," said Wick. Braddy saw him coil his long legs beneath him in order to unkink himself.

"Yeah, mine too."

Braddy Macon was brushing dust from his trousers, smiling and smarting at the same time, watching the faces of the other kids. Envy, he thought. Sore they didn't get to play rodeo on the skidder in place of Wick or me. I'm glad Bannon isn't around. He usually was, standing in the center of his followers, the ones who'd do anything that Leo Bannon ordained. They even laughed, or sort of tried to, if he punched their arms. Why? Bannon wasn't worth that much glory. Even though, when he took a foul shot during a basketball game, he'd first kiss his medal, the one around his neck on a silver chain. Leo pretended to be so all-fired holy. But did Leo ever throw a snowball that didn't have a rock inside?

"Hey," said Wick, "here comes your gal friend."

Braddy Macon tried not to let it happen, but it always did. Something twitched in the empty region between his chest and stomach. Like an echo, every time he saw Sally Rowe. She was walking toward him as if she wasn't in too much of a hurry. What a walk. Sleepy, as though she just got out of bed. And with bouncing breasts beneath her lavender sweater.

"Hi," she said softly.

"Hi yourself."

"Are you walking home with me, Braddy?"

"S'pose so, if I can't locate anyone else."

Sally's eyes widened. She wouldn't hurry a comeback. Never did. All she had to do was *look* at any boy, and he'd melt into a puddle of warm Jello. I want to kiss you, Sally Rowe, he was thinking. Damn, I can't understand myself, because I don't like you that much. But I want to kiss your beautiful face and see your eyes close, and feel your lovely lips say things into my mouth in words I can never seem to hear.

"No one's *making* you walk me home, Braddy."

"Nobody could."

"Plenty of boys *want* to."

"Then take your pick."

"You liked it yesterday. Didn't you?"

Braddy grinned. "Sure and certain."

Sally moved a step closer, to whisper, "So did I."

"I'm sorry, Sally."

"Better be."

Wick Smith came over to where Sally and Braddy stood. "Hey," he said, "let's stop off at the Gulf station and uncap a cold soda pop."

Braddy Macon felt Sally look at him as though she expected him to tell Wicker Smith to bug out. He wouldn't do it. Old Wick was too good a pal.

"No time, Wick. I gotta get home."

"Sally, you want an orange drink?" Wick looked at Sally Rowe as if he hoped she'd say okay, but his face sort of expected she'd turn him down.

"No," she said.

Braddy Macon saw her foot stamp, as if to announce that the afternoon wasn't progressing according to her plan. Wicker Smith retreated a step or two.

"See ya later, Wick."

"See ya, Braddy." Wick left.

"Why don't *you* ever treat me?"

"I would, Sally, but I don't have any cash."

"I do."

"Aw, that wouldn't be fair."

Sally frowned. "Why wouldn't it?"

"Besides, I promised Mom I'd hustle home after school and tote the clean wash across town, back to Mrs. Harrington."

"I see."

"Well, you can come along if you want to help me haul it."

Sally's nose wrinkled. "No thanks. I have better things to do than help you pull some old coaster wagon loaded with a big basket of folded sheets."

"Sorry, but that's my chores. If my mother takes in wash, the least I can do is wagon the baskets."

"How boring."

"Maybe to you. But it's my job."

"Don't you hate doing it?"

"It's not what I'd call pleasure. But I'd hate myself worse if I let Mom do it."

"Doesn't she pay you?"

"Sure, but not in money. Oh, she tries to dish me out a quarter every so often."

"How often?"

"That doesn't matter. Because I won't take it."

"Big brave *you*."

"Yup, big brave me, the coaster-wagon hero."

"You are the most *contrary* boy in the whole school."

"Thanks."

"Why don't you ever want to *go* anywhere or *do* anything?" Ever so slightly, Sally Rowe stamped her foot again.

"Because I'm a monster. That's how I amuse myself. Bradford Macon, the village villain. Watch out, folks, or he'll use his coaster wagon to ram you off the sidewalk."

"You're lucky. You're so *lucky* that you don't even know it."

"Lucky old me." Reaching down to the bench, Braddy picked up his biology book and history book. "Guess I best get going. Laundry awaits."

"Adam Corwin asked me out."

"Bully for Adam Corwin."

"He tried to kiss me, plenty of times. But I won't let him do it. And he's taller than you are."

"Okay, next time I kiss you, I'll stand on a chair. Or a table. Then you can close your eyes and pretend I'm Adam Corwin."

"You think you're so clever."

Braddy grinned. "Sally, I don't mean to be. Honest. I just get a kick out of teasing."

"Somebody ought to knock you down from off your high horse, Bradford Macon."

"Good. Then I'll be sweet and humble, like you."

"Huh. Adam told me that I'm the prettiest girl in the school."

"You are. Adam thinks so. Wick thinks so. And so

do I. Trouble is, Sally *you* think so, too. Ever since we were in the first grade together, you always got the leading part in every play—Snow White, Cinderella, Sleeping Beauty. I'm not saying that you didn't deserve the honor. You're a born star."

Sally smirked. "Thanks a bag."

"You always had the nicest blond hair and the prettiest face. No contest."

"What are you trying to say, Braddy?"

"Nothing. Except maybe you ought to set your sights for a golden chariot and a real prince, instead of a shortstop with a laundry cart."

"Why do I get so *mad* at you?"

"Come on, let's walk some and we'll both work off our temper."

They walked along in the April afternoon, listening to a robin with a twig in its bill. The shortcut through Mrs. Harvey's woodlot contained several large trees, and they both stopped to stand near the trunk of the oldest oak, looking at each other.

"Remember yesterday, Braddy?"

"I kissed you. For the first time and on this very spot."

"Do you want me to be your girl?"

"Only if you want to be."

"When are you going to be fifteen? I'm fifteen already. When's your birthday?"

"In May, on the nineteenth." Braddy Macon

dropped his books, crackling the dry brown leaves beneath their feet. "You *are* pretty, Sally." Placing his hands gently on her cheeks, he drew her face close to his. "And I remembered yesterday all day today. Kissing you is worth remembering forever."

I still can't believe all this, he thought, closing his eyes to slowly meet her mouth with his own. Her arms encircled his neck. Is it true? Am I really kissing Sally Rowe? His knees felt as though they were about to buckle.

Braddy wondered . . . are we in love?

2

"CLUNIE!"

Hearing the voices calling her name, Clunie Finn covered her ears with both hands. She started to walk as fast as she could, being careful not to fall. My legs are too big to run fast, she thought. Papa say I eat too much, and I mustn't eat after school anymore. Not even one Oreo.

"Clunie Finn . . . Clunie Finn."

Not daring to look back over her shoulder, she broke into a trot, feeling her big body bounce with each step. The sidewalk was slate, square after square of different colors. Pretty colors, too, if you have the time to walk slow and look at each one. But now there was no time to watch the colors change from slate to slate. Three mean boys were behind her.

"Clunie Finn, Clunie Finn . . . Lock her up in a loony bin."

As she trotted, she heard the voices gaining, getting closer with every chant. Why, she wondered, do they follow me home from school? Why can't they leave me alone?

"Run faster, Clunie!"

Even with her hands over her ears, she knew that awful voice. His yell was louder than the other voices. He was the one who always started singing the mean song about a loony bin.

I hate Leo.

Although she felt her dress begin to get wet under her arms, she continued to trot, trying to jump over the muddy cracks that separated the slates of the sidewalk. I mustn't fall down. Today was bad in school, when I fall down the stairs. Oh, how I hate my shoes. Papa say I have to wear high shoes because my ankles are weak.

"Clunie's loony . . . lock her up."

I hate Leo. Today I hate school, and I hate my ugly shoes. But I can't wear shoes like the other girls wear. Why do some girls be born like Sally? And why do I always have to be Clunie Finn?

Her eardrums hurt because the palms of her hands were pushing so hard against the sides of her head. I want to hit Leo, but Papa say it's bad to do that. Pa say that I so much bigger than the little children I can't hit back. Because if I hit, I hurt somebody real bad, so bad that the county might put me away in that place. So I don't never hit.

"Clunie Finn, Clunie Finn . . . Lock her up in a loony bin."

I must keep running. I can't hit, she thought. But I can hate. Leo Bannon can't stop me. Never. I'm glad nobody was looking in the hall today when I sneak up to the wallboard and spit on his picture. All my spit ran down his face. He couldn't even wipe it off because it was only Leo's picture.

From behind, Clunie felt a sudden yank at her hair. The pain shot into her scalp, tilting back her head. Screaming, she could no longer see the slate walk, and the toe of her big shoe caught an edge. Clunie fell, her heavy body thudding into a dark purple slab of slate as the cold hardness suddenly met her face. And her knee.

"Fatty legs! Fatty legs! Look at Clunie's fatty legs."

Trying to pull her dress down over her knees, she felt a sharp pain in her hip. Why, she wondered, do I always have to fall down so much? "Don't fall, Clunie. Careful now, and go real slow." That was what Aunt Ida used to say. Ida was Papa's sister. But now she's dead. We buried her right next to Mama. Now there's just Clunie and Papa.

Looking up from the slate walk, Clunie saw Leo smiling down at her. There wasn't any spit on his real face. He knows I did it at school today. Somebody saw. They ran and told Teacher and Leo. But they didn't find me, after the spit. I hid in the furnace room, way down behind the coal, until Mr. Fortino finded me. That was when Teacher made me wash my hands, and I couldn't play with Cal. In our room, there's only two kids: Cal and me. They call it the Special Room.

"Pull up your dress, Clunie."

"No." Clunie made a face at Leo. "I don't want to." And she held her dress tight down over her legs. "I just want to go home and see the ducks."

Leo Bannon squatted down beside her, to whisper. "If you pull up your dress and show me how white your legs are, I'll chase the other guys off. They won't pester you no more."

"No."

"Why not?"

"Leave me be. I want to go home."

"Do you want me to go home with you?"

"No. I don't like you."

"I know a shortcut, Clunie. We can cut through Shattuck's old barn and jump in the hay." As he spoke, Leo turned to grin over his shoulder at two other boys. "We can all go. It'll be real fun."

While Leo's back was turned, Clunie got to her feet

and started to run again. Her shoes felt heavy. She hated the way she had to try so hard. Even so, she could never run fast.

"I going to hide," she said, panting.

Clunie didn't look back. Yet she thought that Leo would follow. Where could she hide? To her left, two houses were close together, forming a narrow alley into which she turned. Running, she scraped her shoulder against the rough clapboards, but didn't stop until she reached the back yard.

Maybe I'm doing something bad, she thought. Papa say to always walk straight home from school, and not to go near the dam or down by the river. Because I don't know how to swim and the dam is a bad place. I have to keep clear of all the danger places.

"Clunie!"

She heard the three boys yelling her name again, but she was too tired to run, and her hip was hurting. The bone was being mean again, like it sometimes did. And her knee felt stiff.

"Here we come, Clunie."

Hide yourself, Clunie. She saw an old hen coop, with busted windows that held sharp bits of glass framing the dark holes, like stars. But the hen coop didn't have any chickens in it. She could hide in there. Where Mr. Fortino, the school janitor, wouldn't find her.

Inside, she saw spiders. Clunie wasn't afraid of bugs

or flies or toads, or anything soft like an animal. Or a doll. The voices were coming again. "But," she said, "I'm not going to hit Leo even if he hits me."

Slam!

The hen coop was dark. Hollering, she moved—stumbling into the web of a spider, feeling the strands of silver tickle her face. Again she yelled. They had locked her inside. The door was shut solid.

"No! Please don't lock me up. I hate it so much."

"We gotcha, Clunie."

"Yeah, we got you shut up in a jail where you oughta be. And you'll never get out. You're in a loony bin."

Pushing hard against the inside of the door didn't help. Clunie felt splinters of rotten wood stab into her hands. Her shin barked against something hard and rusty smelling as she fought her way toward the broken panes of window. Fragments of glass shattered into her fingers, causing blood to run along her wrists in thin red riverlets.

"Let me out!"

I don't want to die, she thought. And this is where I could die. Mr. Fortino won't come. And Teacher won't wash my hands the way she did when they were all black from the coal dust.

"Please . . . please . . ."

Faces looked at her through the small patches of broken window. Leo stuck out his tongue and made a bad noise, a bathroom sound that was even meaner than his face.

"I won't hit," she said.

"You can't do *nothing*," said Leo.

Now there was blood on all the jagged edges of the broken glass, and her hands were burning hot. She thought, I don't like it in this place. I'm afraid to get shut up in a room I can't run away from.

Again her palms covered her ears to help deafen the chanting voices of the three boys. As she did so, she heard a fourth person, a voice that sounded stronger than Leo's or his two friends'.

"Damn you, Bannon."

"Aw, beat it, Macon."

"Yeah, Macon—scram. Go home and soak your head in your ma's washtub."

"Open the door, Bannon."

"Make me. The only thing you could lick is a wound."

"Get out of my way, Leo, or I just might make you sorry."

"You and what army?"

"Braddy! Braddy, I'm in here. Let me out, Braddy. Please . . ."

"I will, Clunie, Don't be afraid."

Clunie heard Leo say, "Braddy Macon, I can whup the tar out of you, and you cussed well know it."

"I know it. But pickin' on me is one thing. Gangin' up on Clunie Finn don't take a bellyful of guts."

"Whatcha going to do about it?" Leo said.

"You got ten seconds to open that door, or every kid in the school will know about this come tomorrow."

"You're a rat-mouth squealer."

"When it comes to something like this, you can bet your butt I am. Coach'll know it. Sally will, too. And she'll tell every ear that'll listen."

"You stink, Macon."

"You'll stink worse come morning."

"I'd like to break your face, Macon."

"Yeah, you probable would."

Bannon opened the creaking door.

3 🌿

PATRICK FINN SQUINTED.

"Dang that girl," he said aloud at the two distant figures walking up the dusty road. Standing in the door of his barn, Pat Finn could see that one of the children was his daughter. Nobody walked quite like Clunie. But who's the other?

"I tell her. A hundred times, I say not to bring nobody home. Just me and her is enough. We don't need no strangers, no townsfolk coming out here to churn trouble."

Patrick Finn could hear their voices, causing him to cup an ear to pick up what he could if the wind blew their words his way. A boy was walking home with Clunie. A cussed boy! God, he prayed, don't let it happen. She's sixteen, and I can't let her go to school no more. So now she's late getting home.

"Grief," he mumbled.

Clunie'll come to it, or the grief'll find her. Maybe the worst is already done. And that boy alongside her, is he the one? Lord, protect her.

"Good-bye, Clunie." Patrick Finn heard the young male voice. "See you tomorrow at school."

Damn young coward! The dirty little whelp musta seen me standing here with a fork in hand, and he don't have the gumption to step forward and face a growed man.

This ends it. No more schooling for Clunie. She grows pretty. But she can't learn no more there than here on the farm. All she's to learn in town is the Devil's lesson.

"Ripe," he said. Sixteen, and a woman for more'n a year now. More like two or three years. But her mind'll ever be childish. Only the Almighty knows why. Me and God both know. Because I was drunk on gin. Shirttail drunk, when I come the road home and tell to bed with Bess. I deserve my torment, Lord.

"Papa!"

"I'm here, girl. Right here. Don't you run, Clunie." Leaning the manure fork against the door frame, he walked a few steps forward on the gravel to meet her. "I know you got things to tell me."

"Papa . . . Papa . . ."

Her arms were around his neck. Closing his eyes, he prayed. Not for God to forgive his sin. No, he thought. This is my reward, my earthly Judgment for conceiving this dull child with Bess. Please, O Lord, punish *me* and not Clunie. You took Bess from me. And I'll bear my burden. I'll bear.

"Clunie you're my precious."

"I be?"

"'Deed you be, child. And all the riches I'll ask for."

If only, he thought, if only . . .

Patrick Finn tried not to remember the evening he'd found Bess hanging in the barn, her bare feet high in the air, whiter than ghosts, slowly twisting around and around on the rope she'd tied to the haybarn rafter. Bess knew that Clunie wasn't right. Not for the first two or three years. But after that they both knew. They'd begot a simple child.

"How is school, Clunie?"

"Good. They let me color now. I promise Teacher I won't no more chew on the crayons."

He hugged her tighter. "Lord love you, Clunie."

"You love me too, Papa."

As her head rested on the shoulder of his faded-blue workshirt, he knew she couldn't see him biting his own lip. So's his chin wouldn't tremble. "My little Clunie."

"I'm big now. More bigger than the other kids. And I hate so much I spit to his face. In the hall."

"Who?" Pat Finn held his breath. She spat on that boy's face and still he follows her to home? Damn that young scamp.

"Who?" he asked her once more.

"Leo."

"Is that him? Is that the boy what walked home with you as far as the gate and then run off?"

"No, that ain't Leo."

"Who then?"

"Braddy."

"You mean Florence Macon's boy?"

"Yes. Braddy is my friend. I love him."

Patrick Finn released his arms from around Clunie, stepping back to look at his daughter's face. And her belly.

"How come he run off?"

"Braddy got chores to do. He told so. And he hate Leo, too."

"Are you hurt?" As Clunie held up her hands for him to kiss, he saw the white scuff marks on her palms. "You fall down, Clunie? There's cuts on your hands, and dried blood."

"I fall down."

"Somebody push you down? Who?"

"They always push me down. Lots."

Patrick Finn sighed. "You're sixteen. And the law says you don't have to go to school no more. Tomorrow you'll stay to home and help me work the place. And we'll get the poles and go up-crick and hook some trout. Or shiners in the dam."

"I can't see Braddy?"

Damnation! Is this the seed of it? Is this Braddy brat

become some sort of a hero in her simple mind? And now she'll *trust* him. He'll do his way with her.

"No, Clunie. You won't have to see nobody. Only me. Just your pa."

"Some days I like school."

"I know. Your teacher done plenty for you, Clunie. More'n I'd ever give her credit, years back. She done plenty for you, and for Cal."

"Cal wet his pants."

"Well, never you mind. You won't have to smell that no more, long as you keep to home. Right here to home, child."

Bending over, she rubbed her knee, causing him to notice the pink scrape on her kneecap.

"I hate that old place."

"You hate the schoolhouse, Clunie?"

"No. I hate the bad place. I hided, Papa. I hided in the furnace room, and then I hided where the spiders live."

"Where?"

"In the bad place, where there's no more hens and the glass is all broke. It cutted my fingers. Braddy wiped 'em."

"He did?"

Clunie nodded, her face intently serious, as if she wanted her father to understand that Braddy Macon had befriended her.

"I love Braddy."

Patrick Finn scowled. "No."

"He smaller than me. But Braddy not afraid of Leo."

"Who is Leo?"

"I hate Leo 'cause of what he done to me."

In Patrick Finn's throat, all his questions seemed to be stuck and lodged, unable to bust out or be heard, or answered.

"Braddy was the one," said Clunie.

"Tell me what he done, girl."

"They wanted me to pull up my dress."

Curse their souls! And to believe, Pat thought, that one of them had the nerve to follow her home. Until he caught sight of me and hightailed it downroad. If I see Florence Macon . . .

"Did they touch you, Clunie?"

"Yes."

"Where?"

"On the sidewalk."

"Talk sense, child. Try."

"They pull my hair, and I fall down. My hip hurts. I want to color in the kitchen. And see the ducks."

"No more, Clunie."

She looked at him without expression.

"Not tomorrow, girl. No more school for you."

"All kids go."

"You're not like all kids, Clunie. You're special. You and Cal."

"I want to be like all kids."

Pat Finn nodded. "Yes, I know you do."

"And I don't want to wear no high shoes. I hate 'em." Sitting down in the gravel of the barn road, she pulled off both her over-the-ankle shoes, the kind she had always worn.

"Maybe it'll turn warm tomorrow, Clunie, and you and me'll both kick off our shoes and wade the brook."

"We *can?*"

"You bet. April water's cold. And this early it'll be slight warmer than ice, but I'll do 'er if you will." He smiled at his daughter.

"I will, Papa,"

"No school. We'll take ourselfs a sweet old wade, instead of."

Clunie shook her head.

"What's the trouble, Clunie?"

"If'n I miss school, you got to write a note to Teacher. I don't want to miss. I'll go barefoot."

"Damn it, Clunie, you'll do as I say."

"Are you mad, Papa?"

Patrick Finn clenched his fists, thinking about Braddy Macon and that Leo kid, and how they wanted Clunie to pull up her dress. What kind of children do people raise nowadays? What kind of varmints live in this town? People don't believe in nothing anymore, or respect anything. Bums. He watched Clunie as she carried her shoes, barefoot on the early April grass, up the knoll and toward the kitchen door.

"Clunie?"

"Yes, Papa . . ."

"Stay clear of the stove, hear?"

"I hear."

Standing near the doorway to his barn, he watched her until she entered the house. The storm door banged as she closed it. She was out of sight, yet he could still see her clumsy walk, almost a stagger; like she'd always be falling down, even when he wasn't nearby to lift her up again. And then dry her tears.

Reaching for the manure fork, he raised it high, ramming the flat tines into the ground beneath his feet with all his force.

"Damn this world."

4

"I'LL GET EVEN."

On his way home, cutting across the town dump, Leo Bannon bent to pick up a dark green beer bottle, quart size. He balanced the bottle on the crest of a rusted car fender.

Yet his thoughts had little to do with beer bottles, or with baseball. Leo was thinking about the sport he could have had with Clunie Finn, until angel-face Braddy Macon had to come along and poke his nose in. I got to get even with Clunie for spitting on my picture.

Backing away from the glass target, Leo had to laugh, thinking about how he'd beaten both Wicker Smith and Gil White for team captain. And how he'd nominated Wick, and gotten Alf Patnode to nominate Gil. Which meant, of course, that Leo had split the votes of the opposition. I'd have lost, he thought, had I run against either one of them.

"Maybe I oughta go in for politics."

Fingers rooting in the carpet of trash at his feet, Leo unearthed a large bolt. He guessed its weight to be about a pound. It felt heftier than a baseball. Trying to squeeze the iron caused the freckles to redden on the back of his right hand.

"One throw. That's all he's going to take, folks. Yes, ladies and gentlemen, the famous veteran catcher of Central High will now attempt the impossible. Not one other kid in town could do it. Except for the great Leo Francis Bannon, the hero of the whole school, as well as the new baseball captain. Leo, you got anything to say to our radio audience before attempting this impossible toss?"

Leo spat. Looking around, he wondered if anyone was hiding nearby, listening in on his imaginary stardom. The dump was deserted.

"Okay, folks," he said, speaking in the nasal twang of a baseball broadcaster, "this here is it. The big moment."

Retreating a few steps, Leo was now about twenty feet away from the fender that supported the green beer bottle. He wondered if he was too far away to give himself a chance. Advancing a yard, he shaved the distance.

His ears heard them all cheering, every kid at

school, plus the people in town. Yelling his name, waving triangular pennants that read LEO in red, white, and blue. A band was almost playing.

"And now, folks, Bannon looks ready. If he smashes the bottle on one throw, he gets the trophy, awarded by this lovely little lady who is now standing here at my side. Her name is Sally Rowe, ladies and gentlemen, and it's real plain to see how she's got the hots for Captain Leo Bannon."

Leo took a deep breath.

Closing his eyes, he tried to picture Sally Rowe holding an enormous silver trophy. Its crest was a figure of a baseball player, a catcher in uniform, squatting behind home plate. The tiny catcher wore an 8 on his back, Leo's number.

"See that, folks? Miss Sally Rowe just blew a good-luck kiss to Leo Bannon, and you all know what that means."

Leo's fingers tightened on the bolt. Using his thumbnail, he flicked a gob of dried mud from under the hexagonal head, and then his fingernail clicked from one thread groove to the next.

"No chance. Not even a slim possibility, folks. Nobody could hope to make a throw like this. Only one guy in the whole world could dare to even try."

Again, in his mind, he saw Sally Rowe blow a kiss at him. Then, with no warning, he saw her father pulling her away, ordering her to go home. Leo felt the bolt harden in his fist. His arm cocked into a hammer, heavy and hard. Nearing where he imagined Mr. Rowe stood in a gray suit that cost plenty of bucks, Leo didn't stop. Not even when he thought he heard Sally's father order him back.

Leo smiled.

Fear! That was what he longed to see on Mr. Rowe's face. So that his cheeks would become as pale as the collar of his fancy white shirt. How could any dude who works in a paper mill wear such sissy duds? Who does this guy Rowe think he is? Just one more bigshot.

"Leo!"

In his mind he heard his own father's voice yelling at him, warning him not to cause any trouble or he'd lose his job in the mill. "You're only a Bannon, kid. Bannons don't never face up to a Rowe or a White or a Paulson. Not in this town, son."

Inside his fist, the iron felt hot, almost molten, as though Leo could have poured iron from his fingers. Around his knuckles he could almost feel the orange oozing from his constricting grip.

Leo felt sweaty all over.

Once more, he envisioned Sally's old man, pointing a finger at him, telling him to stay behind the dump and not ever to venture where he didn't belong. "Keep away from Maple Avenue. Down off our hill. And don't ever dare to even dream about our daughter, Sally, unless you want to get horsewhipped. Or get your old man fired."

"Shut up, Rowe."

Saying it made Leo laugh. Tossing the bolt in the air, he caught it by rote, without actually looking at it fall. The iron firmed his fist, allowing him to turn to confront Sally's father. Leo couldn't see anything except a worn, discarded, and discolored old mattress. Squinting, he tried to force his mind to see Mr. Rowe again. Or better, to see Sally. His eyelids closed.

He whispered, "I love you, Leo."

Softly, he said the three words again, as Sally would have wanted to say them to him. Close by, right against his ear, so he could feel her lips move, and her hair tickle, just enough to tease his cheek.

"Sally," he said.

He yelled her name at the pile of rubbish, feeling foolish, almost ducking into an old plywood carton that had once housed a kitchen refrigerator.

No, he thought, I won't hide.

"Ladies and gentlemen, Leo Bannon is finally ready." Leo looked at the green beer bottle. Now it looked smaller, no bigger than a milk glass. In his fingers, Leo shifted the iron bolt to his left hand, then back to his right.

"Okay, folks—the hour has come. It's now or never

for Leo Bannon and the baseball championship of the world. If he breaks the beer bottle on one toss, he gets the silver trophy. *And* he gets his girl, Sally Rowe. She used to be Braddy Macon's girl, but not any longer. No, sir."

Between where he stood and where the bottle still commanded the fender, Leo thought he saw Mr. Rowe again. The man's hands were on his hips, a fighting pose, blocking Leo's path. Like a barrier.

Leo socked the empty air.

He saw old man Rowe go down, mouth bleeding, and begging for Leo not to punch him again. The man was weeping, hands held over his face, pleading for Leo's mercy.

Leo Bannon kicked his belly.

Even though his foot felt no impact, he thought he heard the thud of pain. Mr. Rowe was down, curled up, arms holding his own guts in defense.

"Crybaby," Leo called him.

"Leo?"

Smiling, he closed his eyes, straining to hear her voice speaking his name. Hardly ever, in all the years of their going to school together, could he ever recall Sally's saying his name. Stuck-up. That's all she's ever been, and she'll be a snooty-nose snob for the rest of her life.

If he ever asked her a question, Sally would answer;

but that was the sum of it. Never had she asked him for anything. Not even when they were supposed to be on the same social studies team. But that wasn't all.

"Happy birthday, Sally."

October second. That was Sally's birthday, Leo knew. Always a party at the Rowe's. Year after year, Leo had run up Maple Avenue hill just to hide in the hedge, after dark, and look in her window. And there they'd be, on each birthday, almost all the kids in the class that were the sharp ones. It made Leo feel as if Clunie Finn and Cal and Leo Bannon were left out on purpose.

When they once had sung the "Happy Birthday to You" song to Sally, he had tried to sing from the outdoors, but the words choked him. And during one chorus he threw up, alone and in the dark of the Rowe's hedge, where no one was there to steady his head or give him something to rinse out his sour mouth.

Why?

Today I saw her looking at Braddy Macon, he thought, staring at him as if *he* was the team captain instead of me. Damn his eyes.

"Me!" he yelled. "*I'm* the captain!"

He yelled it twice more at the green beer bottle, as though trying to explode it by hollering. Some singer, he had once read, could do that—shatter a fancy drinking glass just by singing at it. He wished he could break up a birthday party the same way. Crawl up to the window and scream all of those stinking snobs into fragments. So they'd look like the windshield of a smashed-up car. He could total 'em all. Every damn one.

"Folks, today is Leo Bannon's birthday. And is he going to get a party? Hell, no! Because nobody even knows. Maybe he'll get home in time to find his pa still sober, and maybe his ma will bake him a big white cake, with *Leo* on it. And pink candles, all afire, so he can get to blow 'em out."

Make a wish, Leo.

What'll I wish for? Be great if I could change into somebody besides Leo Francis Bannon, and start over in a new house up on Maple Avenue. Yeah, right across the street from the Rowes. Sally and me, we'd study together. And sing. And every evening I'd sit beside her on their porch swing, so we could sway back and forth. And then, in the moonlight, she'd look at just *me*, and smile. And say my name.

What's my wish? I wish Miss Sally Rowe would look my way as if she actually saw me, and flash me just one honest grin. Like I was somebody. Instead of being what I am, a nobody who lives in one of the shacks on the yonder-side of the dump.

"Can you hear me, Sally? Today's my birthday. Are

you going to come crosstown tonight and hide outside my window, and peek in, like you wanted to be invited to my big fancy party?"

Leo kicked an empty gas can.

Who's going to sing "Happy Birthday" tonight? Will my old man do it? Shucks, no. He's so stupid he wouldn't even know the words. And poor Ma's been cleaning house for the Fishers all day. She'll be lucky if she can crawl home and fix supper. So there goes my birthday cake.

Who needs it?

I don't want no damn cake. And if they bake me one, I'll throw it at 'em, pan and all. You can keep it. Because I'm the team captain now, you hear? Right. So let's have some respect. Here comes big Leo Bannon, the new captain of the Central High baseball team. Sally Rowe's newest lover. That's me. Leo Francis Bannon. And don't forget my name. Best you spell it right on my birthday cake, in big letters.

Leo couldn't see the bottle, not until he raked a sleeve across his eyes and blinked his vision dry. Then he saw it. Afternoon sun turned the green of the beer bottle to emerald; fit for royalty.

Was there ever a King Leo? There was a Pope Leo, I know that. Prince Leo, Duke Leo . . . Captain Leo! Yeah, that's me for sure. Leo the lion.

"Ladies and gentlemen, keep back and give Captain Bannon all the room he needs for his famous baseball wind-up. His great peg from home to second, to throw out the fastest baserunner in the big leagues. Who'll it be?"

Ty Cobb maybe. Coach still talks about Ty Cobb like he knew the gent personal. I wish I knew somebody.

"Folks, get this . . . Mr. Leo Bannon has invited us all to his home, to a birthday party held in his honor; at his house, up on Maple Avenue. And this beautiful green emerald bottle will be his gift, presented to him in a velvet box, with leather around the outside. And his initials, LFB."

Cocking back his arm, Leo Bannon threw the iron bolt at the green beer bottle. He threw so hard, so suddenly, that the jolt made his arm hurt.

He missed.

5 🌿

"I'M HOME."

"You're late, boy."

"I'm sorry, Mama. Honest."

"Supper's cold. I reheated it. Bad enough you don't come home after school's out. Then it takes you to near six o'clock to deliver the wash. But I thank you, Braddy. You're an honest help to me these days."

Reaching into the side pocket of his corduroy trousers, Braddy Macon pulled out three crumpled bills, placing them in his mother's red and shiny fingers.

"Only three dollars," he said.

"We can spend it."

"Reckon we will. What's for supper?"

"Stew."

"Smells rightful good."

Braddy watched his mother pocket the money in her apron. Then Florence Macon moved to the stove, lifting a lid from the steaming black stewpot. "Ain't much meat in it. Mostly potato, and some carrots. But it'll add some grow to your bones."

At the sink, Braddy washed his hands, drying them on a pink and white checkerboard towel. They sat at a kitchen table covered with a cracked and faded oilcloth. Braddy's fingers found his fork.

"Please bow your head for the blessing, son."

Braddy did so.

"Lord," said his mother, "we ask Thee to grace this food for our use, and bless us for all Thy purpose. Amen."

"Amen. This sure looks good, Mama."

"Don't burn your mouth."

On his tongue, the stew was hot and heavy with spice. All he could taste was potato, bits of onion, and sage. The warmth crept into his stomach.

"We dragged the diamond today."

"At school?"

"Yup. I rode the skidder with Wick."

"Wish I could see ya play, Braddy. I bet you're a good baseballer, that is if'n I can believe what the folks in town tell me."

Braddy smiled. "Don't swallow down everything you hear, Mama."

"Someday I'll see a game. Before you graduate."

"Promise?"

"I swear I'll try to."

His mother's face looked tired, Braddy thought, as if all the energy in her thin body had been soaped and boiled out of her. As though she'd been ironed flat. Her face was plain and clean of makeup or lipstick, things she didn't ever buy or use. Not even on Sunday morning. And for her, there was no Saturday night, except for once in a while when she'd walk downtown to hear the band concert. Or see fireworks in July.

"You look tired, Mama."

"That just 'cause I'm lean and old. Still, I reckon I got myself more gumption than any pair of fat folks in this town."

"Reckon you do."

"Washing ain't no delight. Not to yoke to every day. But I s'pose it's better than lots of other jobs. Leastwise, we make out. Don't we, Braddy?"

"Sure enough do."

"We keep a roof above our heads, and the wolf from the door. And that, son, is more than some enjoy. Enough to kneel grateful."

"I want to get a job, Mama."

"Well, you will come summer."

"No, I mean after school, on days when there's no practice. Or on Saturdays."

Florence Macon shook her head. "You worked all fall, while the other lads practiced their football. And into winter, too. We got money put by. Enough to see us through spring and into June. Now don't slurp from your spoon."

"Sorry."

"Manners are important. That is, if you plan to get anywheres in the world, and amount to something."

"I don't know what I want to be yet. It sort of worries me."

"Why should it?"

"Well, it does, because Wick Smith already knows he's going to be a vet, like his daddy."

"Your pa worked in the paper mill. Started at fifteen, not much older than you, and never quit. Even worked his vacation. More'n once. And I won't see you do it."

As her fingers clenched into a small red fist, Braddy thought she was preparing to punch the supper table. Instead, her hand relaxed as she reached for the salt. "Not much flavor in this stew."

"It's savory enough for your favorite shortstop. If you weren't feeding me proper, I wouldn't even sit on the bench."

"You look so skinny and poorly."

Braddy Macon smiled. "Thin people are strong. Isn't that what you just told me?"

The corners of her mouth teased at a smile, but a real grin just didn't ever blossom her face anymore, he thought. My mother's world is all soil and suds and somebody's sweaty socks. Maybe I shouldn't have walked all the way home with Clunie Finn.

Damn! He thought of Leo Bannon.

I wish I had the guts to crack him one on the jaw. Maybe my mother's right. I don't eat enough. Before I go to bed, I'll stuff three slices of bread in me, every night from now on. Until I can balance Bannon.

In his mouth, the tarnished spoon felt hard and hot, as mouthfuls of stew quickly filled his hunger. The supper had plenty of flavor. But the taste I like best, he thought, comes when I kiss Sally Rowe. His mind kept saying her name—Sally, Sally, Sally—as if walking home with her, strolling under the red treebuds of April, was his most important act. Her mouth tasted sweeter than cider.

I wish I were older than Sally Rowe, he thought; and an inch or two taller. Sally was shorter than he was, Braddy knew, but not by much.

Braddy Macon sighed at his stew.

"Deep thoughts?"

"Yes, Mama. Some very deep thoughts."

"I s'pose about baseball."

"Yes'm," he lied. "How'd you guess?"

His mother's voice was stiff, as though her throat

had been starched like a shirt collar. "Guess I know my boy. My shortstop. Come spring, baseball's all that ever occupies your mind."

"This year," he told her, "is my big chance to play short, now that Will Dickle graduated. I'm only a sophomore, but there's no one else. Gil is tight at third. And at second, Andy. He's the best second sacker a team could have. Really anchors the pivot on a double play."

"That's real nice."

"Mama, let me clean up the supper dishes. Okay?"

"What about your studies?"

How do I tell my mother, Braddy thought, how impossible it is to think about Bunker Hill, or cells dividing, when all I can think about is Sally Rowe? She must have the world's most beautiful eyes, and hair; and the lazy way she *walks*.

"Don't worry about my homework. I always do it. Can't get A's unless you hit the books."

Florence Macon got up slowly from the table, pushing herself upward with thin arms. Crossing the kitchen, she carried their two plates over to the tin sink. "I'll wash, and you dry."

Braddy said, "You got it." He wondered if Clunie and her father do up their supper dishes together. Braddy hoped they did.

"You seem far away, boy."

"Me?"

"Like there's something eating on your mind that runs a bit darker than baseball."

"Nope."

"Ya can't fool me."

"Reckon I can't."

As he wiped the dripping supper plate his mother handed him from the dishpan of suds, Braddy Macon wanted to tell her about Clunie. I reckon she knows Mr. Finn, as most people in this town know everyone else.

"More than baseball," his mother said again.

"You're right."

"Well?"

"It's about Clunie Finn."

Florence Macon looked at her son as suds drained from a white coffee mug that she held motionless over the dishpan. "You mean Pat Finn's girl?"

"Yes'm."

"She still going to school?"

"Every day. She and Cal are in Special Class. You know, because of the way they are."

"A crying pity." His mother shook her head, holding her mouth firm in a tight line.

"You mean because Clunie's so backward?"

"More'n that, boy. Guess I was recalling how Patrick Finn found his wife, years and years back, hanging in their haybarn in a loop of rope."

Braddy Macon swallowed. "I didn't know that."

"Pat Finn's had a sorry life. First his drink, and the baby girl that wasn't normal, then the hanging. A sorry life."

"Wow."

"Some folks hereabouts speak ill of Pat Finn, but they'd speak ill of Jesus and The Twelve. Some say Pat's sour and all. Guess he is. And I reckon I know why."

"I saw Mr. Finn today."

"You *saw* Pat?"

"Sure. Mr. Finn's not exactly invisible."

"Where'd ya see him? He don't hardly come into town much. Where was he at?"

"At his place. Out on the old road."

"What was you doing away out there?"

"Oh, I sort of walked home with Clunie."

"Was today the first time ya did that?"

"Yes'm. And I'll do it again if I have to."

"Don't drip the pan on the floorboards. What do ya think they made dish towels for?"

"Sorry."

"How come ya took home the Finn girl?"

"Because of Leo Bannon and his lovable pals. They were being pesky to Clunie, after school. She'd hid herself in an old hen coop and cut her hands on some busted glass. Clunie's a real mess."

"But you feel a pity."

"Yes, Mama. I downright do."

"You done proud. Ya done what was proper, Braddy."

As the dish towel hung around his neck like a scarf, his mother pulled on the two frayed ends so that he'd duck down to her kiss.

6

LEO BANNON SMILED.

Slouching on the bench in front of Dominic's Shoe Repair, in the center of town, he was drinking a bottle of Orange Crush and watching the Saturday parade of shoppers.

"Look at 'em," Leo said to the bottle. "A bunch of nobodies going nowhere. I'd like to blow this town and not come back. Never see their stupid faces again."

Not now, he quickly remembered. Not yet. I'll finish the school year, like I promised the folks I would, but this is the last. One more year of Central High is more than I can take without throwing up breakfast.

Leo's eyes widened.

Sally Rowe! Here she comes with her ma. Damn it all to hell, but why does her mother have to keep such a tight rein on her? Always has, ever since Sally started to bloom into that perfect shape of hers. Worse yet, every time I walk up Maple Avenue, and stop outside the house, her old man comes busting out on the porch. Tells me to shove off, like I was garbage, as though I'm a hunk of nothing that he can order about.

I hate her old man's guts. Because he threatened to fire my old man. Maybe I'll get to Sally to even up the score. That would settle *his* hash. Wouldn't he flip his gasket if he found out his darling daughter got herself in trouble, in a family way, and the guy who did it to her was me.

Searching quickly beneath the bench, Leo selected the longest cigarette butt he could find, a Camel. He lit it, trying not to cough. He wanted to be smoking when Sally saw him.

"Hurry it up," he said.

A cat appeared, jumping up on the bench beside him. Taking a deep drag, Leo blew a cloud of smoke at the cat's face, causing it to blink and then scurry back into the alley between Dominic's and the adjacent building, Nate's Restaurant.

"Beat it, pussycat."

Mrs. Rowe and Sally were about six stores away, Leo noticed, looking in Kassel's window at all the dumb dresses. Taking their own sweet time. Damn! The butt was burning shorter.

"Come on, baby," Leo said aloud. "Come see Leo and let your chubby ma go try on some size eighty-four. That's it. Forget about Kassel's and keep coming my way."

They were talking. But as a few cars rolled by, engines in low, Leo couldn't hear what Sally was saying to her mother. Bannon saw her point at Kassel's window. Her mother nodded once again at some future stop they probably had to make, farther along Main Street.

"That's it, Rowe. Tell your old lady to bug out and you'll see her later."

Sally sure is pretty in that pink skirt and sweater, he thought. Bare legs, white socks. Sexy little mink. She must have a hundred changes of clothes. I wish she'd be *my* girl. I'm just as good as she is, and I could knock teeth out of Braddy Macon. He knows it and I know it. Sally knows it, too, but to her it don't matter much. Women are a pain in the backside.

She's coming.

"Hey!"

Sally Rowe looked at him with an expressionless face. "Hay's for horses. Or didn't anyone ever bother to tell you about manners?"

"Stuck-up."

"Who cares what *you* think?"

"How come you hate me so much, Sal?"

"Wrong. I don't hate you a bit. Not that much."
She held up a pinch of air. "When I look at you, I
don't feel anything."

"Sure, sure. Doing some shopping?"

"I'm waiting for Mom."

"Yeah?"

Boy, thought Leo, she sure is one hell of a looker.
And she had that same sweet body, or darn near, even
when she was twelve. Well, maybe thirteen. Right
now, I bet if she went out to Hollywood, she'd be a
movie queen.

"I got elected baseball captain." Leo took the last
drag and flicked away the cigarette stub.

"So I hear."

Ignoring him, she passed by the bench, pausing to
push open the heavy door into Dominic's. Before he
could stop himself, his hand grabbed her. North of her
knee. Pinching her leg, Leo felt her satin flesh excite
his hand, wanting to grab all of her and hang on. But
her backward kick ripped from his hold.

"Pig!"

As she spat out the word, the metal edge of her purse
chopped his ear, making him release his all-too-quick
touch of her. She went inside, banging the door,
ringing the customer bell. But even though his ear
smarted, grabbing that sweet shank of hers was worth
it. I could, Leo Bannon thought, take a million
whacks on the ear to do it again.

Ow. His ear stung.

Leo looked at his hand, the place on his palm that had slid up Sally's leg. Oh, that delicious babe. Why isn't she a cheerleader? She sort of dresses like one every day at school. I bet it's because her high and holy parents won't let their darling daughter jump around inside half a skirt. They don't want all the studs in town, like me, gaping at Sally's peachy thighs and licking their lips.

Soon, thought Leo. I gotta love some gal pretty damn soon, before I go crazy. Grownups don't seem to know what it's like. Maybe they did once, but they all forgot it by now. Gee, wasn't Mr. Rowe ever a young buck? Just to touch Sally, real gentle, and kiss her lightly on the nose would give me so much pleasure I'd bust buttons.

"Well," he said aloud, "now I *never* will."

Sally's not a Bannon. She doesn't live near the paper mill, where we do, or even where she'll smell it on a hot summer night. Rowes, people like that, live up on Maple Avenue where Bannons don't hang out.

"Nuts," said Leo aloud.

Who gives a hoot about Sally Rowe? Turning around, cupping hands around his eyes, Leo peeked in the window. I wonder, he thought as he saw them talking, what Sally is telling old Dominic. That I put my big hairy paw on her lily-white leg? No, she wouldn't say that. Sally Rowe is spoiled rotten, but

Rowes don't share secrets. Not with either Dominic or me. Just isn't Sally's style.

Why should I care what she says about me? She can fill every ear on Main Street, and I bet that's what she's aching to do. Rat on me. Tattle it all.

"Hell with you, Sally."

Why in the deuce am I sitting here on this bench? Waiting for Sally and her candy legs to slink out? Who needs her? Huh, not Leo Francis Bannon. I don't need any more early Mass, or school, or snubs from Sally. You can take all the Rowes on Maple Avenue and stick 'em up their own noses.

The door opened.

"Hey! I'm sorry, Sally. Honest."

"I bet."

Leo stood up. Why? he asked himself. Why was he bothering to apologize to Sally Rowe? Was it because of what his pa had told him, that Mr. Rowe was the mill attorney? Pinching his daughter could get some-body fired. A yellow slip inside Pop's final pay envelope.

"Excuse it, Sally. I'll make it up to ya."

"Don't bother."

Closing the door, she dropped a package. Leo stooped to fetch it in order to return it to her waiting hand. Sally didn't bend. Not even an inch. As though she expected him to retrieve it, like a wet spaniel with a dead duck in his mouth.

"Here," he said.

Sally Rowe stared at him. Confronting her always made Leo feel smaller, weaker, as though afraid of some hidden force inside that smooth body that was encased in soft pink wool. He was glad he was bigger than Sally, yet his size made no impression on their relationship. His muscles tightened, but he didn't feel any clout in his arms or legs. Only an empty clawing inside his belly, as though Sally was scratching him without even using her nails. Leo wanted to get even.

"I heard about Braddy Macon."

Even though Sally had started back toward Kassel's, where her mother had gone, she stopped to look over her shoulder at Leo.

"What about him?"

Leo smiled. "You don't know?" He was going to string it out, like a hunk of beefsteak he'd once eaten that was too sweet to even chew up or swallow down.

"I don't care," she said.

Liar, he told himself. Sally cares. Or she wouldn't have twisted her hips around to face him again.

"Everybody in the school knows. Alfred Patnode saw Braddy up on the old road. Him and Clunie Finn."

Sally took a step toward him, lips opening, her face in genuine surprise. Ha! She *doesn't* know. Well, it really wasn't all over the school. Alf told me yesterday, that's all. On the way home from practice.

"What about Clunie Finn?"

Itching! Inside, she's hungry to learn anything about Macon, even if it's an earful of dirt.

"Braddy Macon and Clunie Finn."

Sally Rowe frowned, slightly; not a deep scowl. Yes, thought Leo, this is it. Macon is her soft spot.

"I figured Macon was your new boyfriend. Guess I'm wrong."

"Clunie Finn?"

"If ya don't believe me, Sally, ask Alfred."

"I don't believe anything you say. You or that Alfred Patnode. Not one single solitary word."

"Then ask Braddy."

"I don't have to."

Leo Bannon laughed. "Then you'll be the only kid in the whole school who don't know about Clunie and Braddy."

"You're lying, Leo."

"Am I? Then ask Macon, next time you see him alone, which is probably never."

Saying nothing, Sally turned and walked quickly down the sidewalk, dodging shoppers, almost bumping into old Mrs. Phelps. With a snippy whip of her skirt, she darted into Kassel's, out of his sight.

Leo smiled.

7

"TIGHTER."

"About here?" Braddy moved a step forward.

"No," yelled Coach Hackman, "in closer." He drew unseen circles with his arm. "Keep coming until you're toeing the basepath between second and third. That's it. Now turn around and walk five steps toward left. That's the spot. A bit closer to second base but not too cozy."

"How come?"

"Well," said Coach, "it's like this, Braddy." He cuffed back his black baseball cap that had a white C on it. "You can dart to your left easier, and range farther, because that's your glove hand. Not every shortstop can run to his right and backhand a hot ball."

"Is this okay, Coach?"

Coach Hackman stood on the pitcher's mound,

directing his infield, his old face squinting wrinkles at the afternoon sun. His hand rubbed a gray stubble of beard.

"Yeah, Braddy, that's the spot. But if'n they put a man on first, you hitch over a step to your left a yard closer to second."

Gee, thought Braddy, maybe there's more to playing short than I counted on. "I never knew it was so darn intricate."

Coach grinned. "It ain't. But let's say they single a man on. So's the next batter don't hit into a double play, they signal a hit-and-run, expecting our second baseman to break toward the bag, so they can slap it through the hole to allow their front runner to stretch for third. On account it's a long throw to third from right."

"I understand that much," said Braddy, "but what do I do?"

Coach winked. "This'll be how we cross 'em up. With a man on, Wick or Herbie'll throw hard, so they can't pull to left. Hard and outside. Our second sacker stays in the hole between first and second, and you cover the bag. Got that, shortstop?"

"Yessir," said Braddy.

"Good." Coach mopped his face with a rag. "Ya see, this way we'll at least nail *one*. Maybe not two, seeing as the hit-and-run gives him a jump. So he makes second. At least we got a play on the hitter at first."

"Suppose," asked Braddy, "the hitter pulls the ball between second and third? It'll be wide open if I cover second."

"Yup," said Coach Hackman, "I thought of that. So the third sacker floats to his left soon as he sees the runner break off his lead at first."

"But then if the hitter gets way out in front, and pulls it down the third base line—"

"If that happens," Coach snorted, "we're in dire trouble."

Wick spat into the dust. "Don't you fret, Coach, on account there just isn't going to be anybody on first to worry us that much."

"Oh, yeah?"

Wicker Smith shook his head and grinned. "Not when my hook is breaking."

Coach asked Wick how it broke.

"Down and away. Low, outside, and hotter than a live wire. It would take Babe Ruth himself to do anything more than punch it to right. And probably foul."

Coach Hackman sighed. "That's the spirit. You guys may be ugly, but you ain't shy on confidence."

"Ugly?" said Wick. "Me?"

"Nope," said Coach, "you're beautiful. Every doggone one of ya. This'll be the year we'll show the whole blessed league."

"You mean the pennant, Coach?"

"You're natural right I do. Some of you birds is only sophomores, but you'll fatten out the team. We sure graduated a few big bats last June."

Again and again they practiced infield defense against the hit-and-run, just as Coach Hackman had explained. Kept at it until the old man was satisfied. Wick and Herbie Ellis threw curves to Bannon.

"This just might make me famous!" Braddy heard Coach say. "I'm going to give it a name. Yup, a fancy name. Only defense to a hit-and-run."

"What'll ya call it, Coach?"

"The Hackman Shift," he answered. "Boys, come on in here, so's I don't have to holler my lungs out." Coach coughed, while his players ringed the mound. "Do you lads realize that no manager in the majors ever thought of it? This here'll be a baseball first. We gonna make history. Right here at old Central."

Wick grinned at Braddy. "Hmm, the Hackman Shift. Ya know, Coach, that name sort of belongs on a used car."

"Yeah?" Coach pretended to get sore, but Braddy Macon knew how much the old gent savored horseplay, and some good-natured give and take. "Well, seems to me, you ginks'll supply most of the gas. So, seeing as your lip's got so much cussed energy—three laps around the field."

The guys groaned.

"Huh? Make it four. And if'n I spy a one of ya dogging it, I'll tack on extra."

"Slave driver."

Coach limped down off the mound, gesturing his arms to command running. Bannon was in front of the pack, Braddy Macon noticed. Eager Leo, especially if Coach was watching. But when Coach Hackman disappeared, Bannon cheated a lap.

"Catchers don't have to run," he yelled to the passing players. "All we do is squat and think."

Wick, from the corner of his mouth, said, "Squat and stink."

In the showers, the mist was hot and their echoing yells pierced the steam. Bannon snapped a towel at Braddy, but missed, just before Wicker Smith got him from the opposite flank. It smarted.

"Gotcha," said Wick.

Still wet, Braddy Macon tugged on his clothes, picked up his books, and headed for home. Walking slowly, he felt the newly discovered muscles in his legs and back stiffen with every step. Varsity baseball, he was thinking, was going to be one heck of a lot more exciting than the game they had played back in grade school. Even compared to the freshman team. Playing short for Coach Hackman meant more than just roaming around between second and third, waiting for chances to scoop and throw.

"Boy," said Braddy.

He was hitting too. Big bats, according to Coach, won ballgames. Hardwood against horsehide. Braddy was really meeting the ball, not chopping at it—sort of leveling out his swing. His hands still felt the shock of impact. In his head echoed the sound his bat had made, three times in a row, against Wick. No sound could ever match the whack of a bat against a ball. Each spring, the wood exploded louder and louder, more solid with every swing.

"You're my next shortstop," Coach Hackman had told Braddy a year ago. And, Braddy concluded, it's my bat as well as my glove. Hackman loved hitters. One hit a game. That's all he's asking. "Only one pitch counts," Coach had said, "and that's the *now* pitch. Not the one you just swung and whiffed on. Forget it, because the first two strikes aren't any more than two tiny hashmarks of history that nobody don't recall. It takes three for a K."

"Baseball," said Braddy, grinning to himself, looking at the red maplebuds overhead that wanted to bust out into young leaves.

He heard a robin whistle. He'd take a detour up Maple Avenue past Sally's. Maybe she'd be home. I wonder what their house looks like inside, he thought. There wasn't a boy at Central who didn't know where Sally lived; except maybe for Cal, who probably wouldn't know his own nest, let alone anyone else's.

Poor old Cal.

Turning the corner, Braddy Macon saw a bunch of kids, maybe a dozen or so, gathered in front of the vacant house on Altamont Street. They were shouting, chanting something, and running around in circles. Above their heads, Braddy saw an object wave, which looked like the business end of a janitor's pushbroom. Then he heard the lyrics of the chant:

"*Clunie Finn, Clunie Finn, . . . Lock her up in a loony bin.*"

Braddy Macon forced himself to trot, even though his legs were hurting.

"Hey, what's going on?"

Helen Grinell turned to Braddy. "They got poor Clunie surrounded. Not hurting her or anything, but it's just so mean and cruel. So darn unfair to lean on Clunie all the time."

There, in the center of a ring of young, jeering faces was Clunie, wobbling in her ugly high-top shoes, swinging the pushbroom in giant circles. Her shiny face was pink and sweaty, perhaps wet from more than just perspiration. Some of the kids were Braddy's age, but most of them were younger. Ten, or even nine. It's really great, Braddy thought as he elbowed into the circle, that the little ones can learn the rotten words.

"*Clunie Finn, Clunie Finn, . . . Lock her up in a . . .*"

"Come on, Clunie," he said. "Let's split."

"Braddy? Make 'em quit." Clunie was still trying to swing the pushbroom in circles, in an effort to fight off the ring of hecklers.

"Let's go home, Clunie."

"Make 'em."

"Sure, I'll make 'em quit." Braddy Macon said nothing to any of them. Not a word. He didn't even want to look at their dumb faces. None of them, he thought, were worth a glance. Except for Helen. She was okay. What could one little gal do against a mean mob of rowdies?

Let's go, Clunie. Let me have the broom."

No."

"You could hurt somebody." Braddy's voice was soft and steady as he noticed how flushed Clunie's face was. Fear? Rage? They weren't hurting her at least. Not with kicks or punches or by throwing stones. But don't they *know*? Don't they have any feelings? Some of them backed off.

"Please, Clunie . . . Let me have the broom."

"It mine."

"No, it isn't, Clunie. You just borrowed it from school, remember? And I promise I'll return it tomorrow morning."

"You'll tell."

"No, I won't. Besides, there's nothing to tell. All I'll say is that I had to sweep the walk, and give the broom back to Mr. Fortino."

Braddy saw Clunie's eyes shift. "Don't never give it to *them*."

"I promise."

"Braddy . . . I like you much."

She handed over the broom, and he took it, holding it under his arm along with his books, cutting a gate through the ring of kids. Clunie started to turn around.

"Don't look back."

"I won't, Braddy."

"And don't ever fear a pack of cowards."

"They follow."

"Not this time."

After stowing the broom where he would later retrieve it, Braddy and Clunie walked for nearly an hour, covering the distance slowly in the direction of the Finn farm, unhurried. With each step, Braddy's sneakers waited for the heavy shoes.

"I still glad," Clunie said.

"About what?"

"I won't stop school."

"Atta girl."

"Papa say *no* sometimes. Papa don't want me to school."

"But you like it."

"I like Teacher."

Braddy nodded. "Good going, Clunie."

"I like ducks, too. And crayons. I don't rip off the paper no more."

Braddy held her hand, surprised at her strength. Clunie was a little girl imprisoned in a hefty woman's body. She is stronger than I am, he thought.

"Most of all I like daisies."

"So do I, Clunie."

"When'll they come?"

"Well, it's still April. Daisies don't blossom until May or early June."

"Braddy, you tell me when it's May."

"I won't have to, Clunie."

"Why?"

"Because you'll see all the daisies."

8

"TEACHER GET MAD," SAID CLUNIE.

"At you, or at Cal?"

"Me. I got thirsty."

Braddy said, "There's a water fountain in the hall."

"I know."

"So?"

Clunie smiled. "I drink out the goldfish bowl."

"Don't do that again, Clunie. Please don't."

"Teacher say I might drink the fish."

"No, you wouldn't do that. Imagine what that would be like, with an itty-bitty goldfish flopping inside your tummy. I bet you'd have a tickle you couldn't scratch."

Together they sat on a fallen tree that lay beside the dirt road. Braddy started to worry about the time. Mrs. Harrison would just have to wait for her laundry.

Clunie's more important than her peach-bordered bedsheets.

"You know, Clunie, when I was a little boy, Mama said I stooped over and took a sip out a mudpuddle."

Clunie Finn laughed. Her voice was smooth, and her laughter floated upward sort of like the notes of a shepherd's flute, released to be free, or a flock of little yellow goldfinches. Braddy discovered how much he liked to hear Clunie's joy.

"Will it get May tomorrow?"

"No, but soon."

"Touch my hand again."

"Why?"

"I like it. Papa touch my hand. Lots and lots, before I go to sleep nights."

"I reckon you love your pop."

Clunie nodded.

"Mine's dead. I don't recollect him very much, but my mother tells me all about him. I guess he was an okay guy."

"I'm glad."

Braddy smiled at her, feeling the warmth of her face as she looked at him. The only thing really pretty about Clunie is her eyes, he thought. He tried not to look at her shoes.

"You smile real good, Clunie."

"Thank you."

"I guess I'm sort of happy inside, to be able to say

things that'll make you smile at me. Promise me something?"

"Yes."

"Promise me that you'll smile every day."

"For you, Braddy?"

"Yep. Just for me."

"And not even for Cal, or Teacher."

"Only me. And one more thing."

Clunie waited.

"I don't want the kids picking on you anymore. Not a darn one of 'em."

"They don't stop."

"Never you mind, Clunie. They won't dare to hurt you. Maybe it'll hurt your feelings some, but pay it no mind. Because you know what?"

"What?"

"Clunie, you're *stronger* than they are."

"I know. Papa tolded me."

"Your pa's right. That's why you must *not* pick up things, like a broom or a baseball bat, and start swinging."

"I'll hit'em and hurt."

"Right. And that's bad, Clunie."

"Papa, he said that."

"You could hurt somebody, Clunie, because it's possible that you don't know how strong you are." Braddy felt her arm. "Kid, you got muscles you haven't even used yet. You might even lick Leo."

Braddy Macon saw Clunie's face darken. Bending over, she lifted a thick twig, suddenly halving it with one violent snap.

"Leo," she said, looking down at the broken branch. Gripping it, choking the wood, her knuckles whitened. With a sudden attack, she beat one stick against its former part, but only once.

Braddy felt wet.

"Hey, easy now. Leo's okay."

"No. No okay."

"Don't think about Leo Bannon. After all, why waste an afternoon on that turkey?"

Clunie looked questioning. "Leo's not no turkey."

Braddy smiled. "No. Leo's just Leo. He's not a turkey and he's not a lion. Leo's only a Bannon. Who knows, maybe it's not all Leo's fault he acts so ornery."

On plenty of occasions, Braddy thought, Leo Bannon ought to be put in the Special Room with Clunie and beanpole Cal. Wow, that would *kill* him. Would that ever chop Leo down to size. The thought made him smile.

"You laugh, Braddy."

"Sure do."

"Why? At *me?*"

"No, at Leo. Come on, Clunie, let's the both of us laugh at Leo." Braddy strained out his cheeks so his face would look as round and crimson, and as Irish as he could force it.

"You are funny, Braddy."

"Don't ever be afraid of Leo or his pals, Clunie. We'll just laugh at him, you and me. Laugh at pudgy old Leo until our sides split open. And if he ever gives you any grief, we won't hit Leo. We'll just get Mr. Nash to lean on him some."

"I like Mr. Nash."

"Yeah. Our principal's a good cat."

Clunie laughed. "Mr. Nash is a cat?"

"Well, not exactly. And please, *please* don't tell people I called the principal a cat. I'm in enough trouble."

"I don't tell."

"You're real sweet, Clunie."

Braddy didn't know why he did it, but for some reason he leaned forward and kissed Clunie's cheek. Without thinking, merely because he wanted to do something nice for her, to make her forget the crowd of kids that had encircled her, chanting about locking her up. Clunie's sudden smile polished her face.

"Thank you."

"Gee, I'm sorry, Clunie."

"Do it more."

Braddy stood up. "Come on, we gotta get you home before your pa starts out looking for you, and finds *me*."

"Why?"

"Because people don't always understand everything. They think things real quick. And say a lot of stuff."

"What stuff?"

"Words they don't mean." Braddy took her hand and pulled Clunie up on her feet. "Besides, that old log is too hard for my skinny rump to sit on. Let's cut through your old man's meadow and look for daisy buds on the way home."

"Now?"

"Sure. Right now."

"Is it May?"

"Not quite. But we might be able to see daisy plants in the pasture. We'll find some buds."

"Braddy, you kiss me."

He sighed. "Forget it. It's a secret, Clunie. Sort of like Mr. Nash is a good cat. You can't tell it, okay?"

"Okay."

Braddy held down the bent wire fence so that Clunie could climb over. Gee, he thought, she sure is one meaty girl. I wish she could lend me a few extra pounds.

"Where are the daisies, Braddy?"

"No sweat. We'll find some. Honest. Daisies grow everywhere this time of year. Except maybe down in Argentina where it's fixing to be winter."

"No. Winter's over."

"Right. Please don't run. I'll wait for you, Clunie, and we'll search out a daisy plant."

He found one. Bending low, his hand felt the greenery, dark and tender, jagged leaves that looked like they could go in a salad. And in the center, on stubbly stems, some tiny green buds. Hard little knots of light green; in places, almost the color of cream.

"Look here, Clunie."

"That's not daisy."

"No, not flowers yet. But see these wee little buds? Remember this place now, Clunie. Just north of that flat rock. If you watch these little guys every day, you'll see daisies sprout up. All with yellow suns in the middle and a ring of white petals that sort of look like tiny Indian canoes."

"Honest?"

Braddy laughed. "Honest Injun. And I reckon Injuns are about as honest as the rest of us. Aren't they?"

"Yes."

"Remember now. Every single day you have to check, and then tell me when the very first daisy opens up, all yellowy and white."

"Do they smell?"

"Well, *do* they?"

"No," said Clunie. "Some flowers smell sweet, but not daisy."

She knows more than people think, Braddy Macon told himself. He looked up at her from his hands-and-knees pose on the humpy green of the pasture grass. In spots, the grass appeared darker and richer, no doubt where Mr. Finn's milk cows had dropped manure.

"Braddy?"

"Yes . . ."

"Come see my ducks."

"I want to, Clunie." He knew, as he spoke, that he really did. "But not today. Baseball practice gets me late enough. I gotta go."

"Please . . ."

"Can't do it, Clunie. Some other day. It'll be May soon, and I bet that along with the fresh daisies, you'll get some little yellow ducks."

"On the pond."

"Good."

"Pond got a snapper in it. Snapper turtle."

"In your pond?"

"Yes'm." Clunie laughed. "That's how I answer Teacher. I say yes'm."

"But I'm not your teacher."

Clunie nodded. "You almost be."

"Okay, I'll be your teacher, if you keep all the secrets that we share."

"I'll keep."

"Good. I'm glad you're still in school, Clunie. I can't picture the old place without you, and Cal."

"Come see my ducks. Please."

"I will, Clunie. Real soon."

"Promise."

Braddy Macon raised his right hand, crossed his heart with a finger, and closed his eyes. "I most solemnly swear—"

"Don't swear. It bad."

"I do most solemnly promise to uphold the Constitution, fight injustice, protect the innocent, slay dragons, and rescue fair damsels in distress."

"And—"

"Oh, and I also promise to come see Clunie's ducks."

"When?"

"Soon's I can. On a day when there's no baseball practice. I'll walk home with you, and we'll pick daisies"—Braddy started to back away—"and we can bring a big bouquet to your new baby ducks."

"Thank you."

"Aw," he hollered to her as he vaulted the wire fence, "don't even mention it."

"I like you, Braddy."

"Hey! I like you, too, Clunie. You're okay."

"I like you"—she sounded hesitant, as though the last three words had to struggle to be spoken—"more, more, more."

"More than who?"

Clunie laughed. "More than daisies."

9

"IS IT TRUE?"

Beneath the long table, Sally Rowe stomped the tile floor with the red rubber heel of her loafer. Only once. Aware of her action, she forced her body into control, folding her hands.

"Suppose it is?" asked Braddy from across the table.

"I don't believe it."

Sally wanted to yell at Braddy Macon as he faced her in the lunchroom cafeteria. Though the noise of banging trays and talk disturbed her concentration, Sally was grateful for the background of sound that would help mask her words.

"Look, Sally, there's nothing to believe."

"Leo Bannon told me. The creep. I *would* have to hear all about it from *that* troll. Well, *is* it true or isn't it?"

Sally waited for Braddy to answer, but all he did was gurgle the lower end of his straw in the dregs of the chocolate milk container. It made a disgusting noise.

Braddy Macon finally replied, "I guess it's true enough. Whatever it was that Leo told you must be Gospel, because Bannon wouldn't lie. Not a swell, upstanding eagle scout like Leo."

Sally whispered, "You infuriate me."

"You don't look very furious."

"I never do. A woman can burn inwardly."

"Are you burning?"

"In a way." Sally's hand crumpled her paper napkin into a hard little ball.

"You're ticked."

"Well, I certainly have cause to be."

"How could you get sore merely 'cause I walk home with Clunie?"

"You're always too busy to walk *me* home. Or to go for a soda or something. You and your baseball practice."

"There, there . . ."

"Don't talk that way to me, Braddy. I'm not a child. I'm older than you are."

"In some ways."

Sally watched Braddy tie a knot in his straw. A drop of chocolate milk fell from one end, making a tiny wet star on the cafeteria table. She suppressed her sudden impulse to wipe it away.

"What's *that* supposed to mean?"

Braddy smiled. "Nothing."

"The important elements in your life seem to be baseball, laundry, and Clunie Finn. All I want to know is where *I* fit in."

She saw Braddy let out a deep sigh. For a moment his face seemed to be quite grown-up, as though he couldn't wait to be graduated and working. Out into the world. Behind her, a boy dropped his tray with a soupy and shattering clatter. Why, thought Sally, can't high schools have little rooms where two people can go and be alone? The smell of the lunchroom did little for her appetite. Before her was a half-eaten sandwich. How, she wondered, could anyone be expected to eat in this zoo? It was more like a combat zone.

Braddy said, "Some things are hard to explain."

"Apparently." Sally felt pleased with her one-word remark. I'm more sophisticated than *he'll* ever be. But if that were true, then why am I pressing him? She straightened her spine. Never slouch, she told herself. And keep your hands away from your face. Conversation shouldn't have to lurk behind knuckles.

"Yeah, it's true. Yesterday I walked almost all the way home with Clunie."

"Again?"

"That's right."

"Why do you have to be such a white hat?"

Braddy grinned. "Because."

"That is hardly an answer."

Sally Rowe watched her own hands slowly open the bud of her white napkin ball. She liked her hands with their long and slender fingers.

"Do you like Clunie?"

"Matter of fact, I do. In a different way than I like you, Sally. It's not too simple to talk about. Yet it is, if you'd only stop to think about it."

"I'm thinking."

"Look, I don't want to feel sorry for Clunie, because that's what everybody does. For her and for stringy old Cal. I know, everybody laughs at the pair of them. Me included. But I'm not laughing anymore."

Sally shrugged. "Neither am I."

"Because it's no longer funny. We all used to giggle about it, for years. Like saying Clunie and Cal ought to get married and breed idiots. Start their own funny farm and call it The Clunie Bin."

Braddy was right, thought Sally. His face looked so serious all of a sudden. It's the reason I like him so much. Why do I have to constantly find out if Braddy likes me as much as I like him? Why can't I be cool?

"I expect to see you after school, Braddy."

He grinned at her. "So we can kiss?"

"I don't appreciate being teased."

"Nobody does. Not even Clunie."

"I suppose not."

"And not even Cal. But the difference is that Cal doesn't know when he gets kidded."

"You're saying that Clunie does."

"I sure am. Perception is something you can sense in other people, Sally. You know I have a brain that works, just like I'm aware of yours."

"I bet you're aware of more than my brain."

"Spoken like a true empress."

"You're teasing me again. It's cruel to tease Clunie, but it's okay to tease *me* at every opportunity."

"Sure. You're the invincible Sally Rowe, remember? You're not just a girl. You're a fort."

"Wrong. I can take a jab now and then, providing."

Braddy kept knotting his straw until Sally snatched it from his fingers, throwing it down on her tray. Easy. Lay back, she told herself.

"Who's teasing you, Sally?"

"Everybody. It started with Leo Bannon last Saturday when I was shopping with Mother. Then, all week long, kids come up and mumble things in my ear. After about a dozen times, it makes me wonder, that's all."

"Good."

"Good? You want to be a part of it?"

"No, I really don't. But I'd like to be a part of Clunie Finn."

"Then it's true."

"Sally, you have feelings. So do I. Trouble is, maybe all the kids don't realize that Clunie Finn feels things, too."

"Is that all we're *ever* going to talk about? Clunie Finn?"

"Maybe the time has come, Sally."

"What time?"

"Somebody's gotta do something with Clunie."

"And you're volunteering. My hero."

Her voice had sounded unduly cold, causing Sally to dislike herself. I hate all this, she thought. Why does being with Braddy Macon have to be so complicated?

"You tell me, Sally. If I don't, who will?"

"I give up."

"Maybe it'll be Bannon."

"He's an ape. I bet Leo shaves his palms."

"Right. Leo's an ape. I got a hunch that Bannon might try something with Clunie, and it's not a very pretty picture."

"Clunie's what he deserves."

"*No!*"

Her tray bounced as Braddy Macon's fist pounded the table, and Sally knew that heads had turned to look at her; at both of them. She felt her cheeks color slightly, wanting to get up and march out of the cafeteria, without even turning in her rubbish at the scullery window.

"Keep your voice down, please."

"I'm sorry, Sally."

"And *don't* say you're sorry. My father says it's a sign of weakness. And I guess I knew what you meant, so the apology isn't necessary. I wasn't serious when I said Clunie deserves to get jumped by lurking Leo. *Nobody* deserves that."

"She senses things, Sally. Honest. It's like her brain is trapped inside her, screaming to get out. But nobody'll unbar the door to her dungeon. Clunie's got more on the stick than people think. She's curious about all kinds of stuff."

"Such as?"

"Daisies. Ducks. Can't you see the difference between Clunie and Cal? Poor old Cal wouldn't even know if he was dressed or naked, until he felt cold, and then he'd probably go crawl under a table. You could toss Cal your pink nightie and he'd try to put it on."

"How did you know I wear a pink nightie?"

"I didn't."

"Well, now you do. And I bet you'd like to see me getting into it. Or getting out of it." Sally was surprised at her own nerve, saying something like that.

Braddy Macon swallowed.

That got to him, Sally told herself. Now maybe he'll stop discussing Clunie Finn and Cal for a minute. She felt warm, toasty, as though she were in bed. He's staring at me, she thought. I wonder if boys can read girls' minds. A girl always knows what a guy is thinking. One thing—the big trick.

"Say something, Braddy."

"I can't."

"How come you're so silent?"

"I'm envisioning you."

"I bet."

"Why *me*, Sally? How come I'm the lucky one who gets close to the school's most winsome lady?"

"You're not there yet, buster."

"No. But we're talking about it."

Sally saw Braddy's hand grip the edge of the table, as though he wanted to claw away at something. "And thinking about it." She moistened her lips slowly.

"You're a tease, Sally."

"Right, lover." She almost snarled. "How's it feel?"

"Rotten, and rich. I can't decide which one. Not really rotten. Just painful." Braddy bit his lip.

"Take aspirin."

"It's not that kind of pain."

"What's it like?"

"Like I could punch out a gorilla."

"Try it with Bannon."

"Maybe I will."

"Could you?"

"Aw, who cares if I could or couldn't."

"Braddy, what would you do if I told you that if you

carve up Leo, I'd let you do more than just kiss me?"

Braddy's eyes seemed to darken to an icy blue. He's looking into me, Sally thought, very deeply; yet my eyes are not what he's thinking about. Well, it's not going to be that easy, Braddy. Not even for you.

"Why are you saying all this, Sally? You never told me this before. Not even when I kissed you. You didn't ever say anything like that."

"Maybe not to you."

Sally felt the corners of her mouth begin to smile. Opening her lips, she let herself laugh, silently.

"Please don't, Sally."

"Why not?"

"Because to me you're still Sally Rowe, my star, and I want to look up to you, not just look *at* you. I want you like all hell. So doggone much that I've got the all-over hurts."

Sally smiled.

IO ✿

"CAREFUL NOW, CLUNIE."

"I be careful, Papa."

"Best you do. If'n you stand out too close to the edge of that rock, you could fall yourself in and drown."

"I want to pet the baby ducks."

"Well, now that there seems near to possible, if we let the ducklings come to you."

"They won't come."

"In the barn we still got some ears of corn that've been tacked up. Dried all winter. So I'll crack some corn for you to feed 'em on. Be right back."

Patrick Finn walked to his barn. Removing two of the largest ears, he pulled off the dry husks that were tan and brittle, rubbing one ear against the other until the hard yellowy kernels nearly filled the basin. With a masher, he shattered the kernels into dusty fragments, then returned to Clunie, who was still at the duck pond west of the house. He handed her the wooden bowl.

"Here ya go."

"Thank you, Papa."

Brushing the cream-colored corn powder from his hands, Patrick pulled his daughter gently to his side. Leaning over, he kissed her hair. A soapy smell met his nose, pleasing him that she had washed so thoroughly this morning. Helped him with the breakfast dishes, too. Didn't drop or break a single cup.

"Bless you, Clunie."

"I bless you, Papa."

Pat Finn smiled.

"How do I feed 'em the corn?"

"Oh, I don't guess there's much of a trick to it, not to get ducks to eat up corn. They'll know it by natural."

"Do they?"

"Sure enough do."

"How?"

"Here, I'll just toss a couple three bits into the water. See *that*?"

"The mama duck knows."

"Yup. Witness how she eats up."

"Here come the babies, Papa."

"How many we got this year?"

The tally was plain to Patrick Finn. Their old drake

and duck, one pair, had produced eight eggs in the nest. One got smashed, but seven hatched out. A good yield for a clutch of eight eggs. Maybe, thought Finn, that was because his Clunie so wanted the ducklings to fill the nest they had discovered among the cattails, off to the right, on the north bank.

Matured, the ducklings would be as white as the pair. But now the seven were wee balls of yellow fluff, floating like toys, curious about the cracked corn.

"Here," said Clunie.

She tossed a handful of corn, watching the many particles speckle the water. The old white drake would not eat. All he did, Patrick noticed, was oversee the feeding of his mate and young, quacking his soft little warnings, a constant nag to be cautious.

"We ain't a fox," spoke Finn.

Clunie laughed.

"What's so funny, daughter?"

"You ain't a fox."

"No."

"But that Leo is a turkey. And Mr. Nash . . . he's a good cat."

"Who says?"

"Braddy."

"He brung you home again, eh?"

Clunie nodded. "Oh, Braddy, he is so good. *All* good, Papa."

I wonder, thought Patrick Finn. "Nobody's all good,

Clunie. We're created in the Lord's likeness, but we all be sinners, one way or other."

"You. You all good."

The feeling choked him, as if he couldn't swallow; nor could he drink. No, never again a drink. Nary one lone pull from a jug. Corn was meant to feed ducks and fatten a fall hog. Not for the jug, nor to be uncorked to wet his lips. Over his shoulder, he looked at the barn to remember his wife.

"I paid," he said aloud.

"What?"

"Just talking, darling. A lonely mouth talks to a likewise ear, so they say. Now then, how many we got? Let's count up."

"One, two . . ."

"Three," he prompted her.

"Three . . . five."

"Whoa. Four comes next. Then five."

"Five, six . . ."

"Seven. We got seven ducklings, Clunie, and each one's yellower than new sunshine."

He saw her squint at the sky, looking out over the west meadow, suddenly pointing.

"Papa, it's May."

"It's what, daughter?"

"May. See the daisy? Can't be April no more, so now it's May. May, Papa."

"Who told you that? Your teacher?"

"No. Braddy says."

"Him again."

"Braddy told me to watch the daisy plants. When the flowers come out, it's May."

"Do your friend Braddy like daisies, too?"

Clunie nodded. "And he likes *me*."

"He say so?"

"Yes. Told me so. But I already know." As his daughter spoke, she looked up at him, to smile.

Patrick Finn petted her cheek. To trust nobody, he thought, makes about the same sense as to trust everybody. Maybe I should talk to the Macon boy. Clunie trusts him. That much I already took stock of. Yet it all rubs me. Never cotton up to townfolk, on account there's not a whit of trustworth in the pack. Nope, not even among their young. Too many years I seen Clunie cry her way home from the schoolhouse, assaulted in one manner or other. She's strong, though. Made her tougher than righteous.

"How old is Braddy Macon, girl?"

Clunie shrugged. "I don't know, Papa."

"You like him?"

"A whole lot."

"Good. I'm glad you got friends," he lied. No, he thought, I ain't happy about the none of it. Breeds trouble, the way I figure. All them young tomcats do is chase skirt. Hoot and holler, like every day was Saturday night, the way I used to do. And not a speck of difference between one of them pups and another. Louts, all of 'em. I'd wager that Macon kid is cut from the same bolt.

"See the ducks, Papa?"

"I see 'em, sweet."

Clunie reached down her hand. "They don't pet."

"No, not like a cat. Too skittery. And that be nature's way, girl. Old Mother Nature, she tells all them wee ducklings to keep wary of strangers."

"Why?"

"Well, to keep safe. So if'n a red fox comes to prowl around our pond, they'll all take to the water, and swim out of harm's way. They'll learn to abide the water so's they don't get ate up."

"Papa, will they always be safe?"

"Some."

"Not all?"

Patrick Finn leaned closer to his daughter, watching her chubby hands tossing gems of cracked corn into the pond. "Maybe not all, sugar. But they got my Clunie to watch over 'em, sort of the way that I'll always watch over you."

"Like the mama duck."

Finn nodded.

Just as Clunie screamed, dropping the bowl of corn into the water, he also saw what had terrified her. There he was, the big oval of his muddy back ringed by the jagged edges of his heavy shell. As he swam upward toward the surface of the pond, clawing with his talons, the water around him churned into brown clouds. Opening his strong beak, the big snapping turtle hissed at the ducks.

Clunie screamed again. "No! No!"

Pulling his daughter back from the pond's edge, Patrick Finn searched the ground at his feet for a rock, a stick, anything that would spook the turtle. His hands felt numb and slow.

"Papa! Don't let him."

He could find nothing to throw. And there was no more time. His heart pounded as the cold water beat upon his body, the muddy bottom of the pond sucking at his work shoes. With a clumsy splashing of his arms, he half swam and half yelled his way forward, no longer seeing the giant turtle; yet knowing, knowing.

Ahead of him, the ducklings were scattered by the thrashing of his hands, unaware of the real danger. Patrick could hear the urgent squawking of the male duck, who had seen the turtle. The weight of his shoes seemed to pull him under, yet all his limbs groped through the icy pond in an effort to frighten away the snapper. Clunie screamed and pointed, but he saw no turtle. Muddy water stung his eyes.

"There! Over there, Papa."

Turning his head, Patrick Finn saw the beak open. Too late. The female duck tried to tuck one of her ducklings beneath her white wing, quacking at her offspring, not noticing the head that stabbed at her, snapping faster than a dog.

"Hyah! Git away."

The hooked snout tore at the white feathers. There was a crunch of bone as her wing was caught in his jaws. As both her orange feet kicked at the armored head, her free wing struck at him, yet causing no damage. Her quacking head was yanked beneath the surface, as the snapping turtle and his prey sank once again into the mud at the bottom of the pond.

"Papa! Save her, Papa!"

Twice he dived down into the muddy water—groping with his hands, seeing nothing, coming up only when his lungs felt nearly insane for want of air. Mud, cold water, strangling clothes, and leaden shoes; all prevented Patrick Finn from doing little more than fighting his way to shore, flopping on the bank of thick weeds and algae. Water coughed from his windpipe.

"Clunie . . . I tried, Clunie . . ."

His daughter stood still, hands covering her ears, looking at the spot in the pond that still bubbled with drowning death. Clunie was pointing, crying, silently screaming her terror, somehow knowing that the mother duck could never battle her way to the surface. Deep in the mud below, her white feathery body was being chopped and hacked by a beak tenfold stronger than hers. Her lungs now ached for the air above that would be denied her. Only darkness, water, and death.

As he held his daughter, Patrick could not tell which one of their bodies shook more. Clunie was trembling. Her chin was chattering as though she felt as frozen as her father. The wind bit his wet body.

"Oh, Papa . . ."

"I know, Clunie . . . I know."

"Why did he do it?"

His wet arms wrapped around her, and he didn't care that they both were soaking and cold. She wanted an answer, as always, demanding answers every day for questions that were even more of a mystery to him.

"God just took her, Clunie."

"No. That old snapper ain't God."

"Don't be afraid, girl. What you seen was just a share of the world. Just one share."

"Bring her back, Papa. Bring back my ducky."

"Oh, how I pray I could."

"She dead . . . dead."

"Yes, because the Lord willed that turtles'll eat ducks and ducklings, and there's naught that mortal man can do to change what's been ordained."

"It's so—*mean.*"

"I know, I know." He held his daughter's face close to his dripping shoulder, feeling the shaking of her heartbreak against his wet shirt. The wind felt so cold.

"That turtle's mean, like Leo."

"Don't you question, Clunie. You and me, child, is not to block the ways of the Almighty. It was just her *time*, girl. Her day to die. Best you face it, because my day to meet Judgment'll come and you got to . . . got to be . . ."

Patrick Finn couldn't finish his thought. Hoping that Clunie would die first, because no God in Heaven would be so full of wrath as to take him and leave Clunie to fend for herself. Without their ma, the yellow ducklings might have a chance. But without me, he wondered, what lot would Clunie have? Who'd give her a roof?

"Oh, Papa . . . my heart's all busted up."

"Like mine," he whispered to her.

Looking upward, he saw the overcast sky and all its ashen gray, endless curds of clouds that blotted out the sun. I can't, he told the heavens. I can't take no more torment. The debt's paid, Lord. I'm paid up.

"Come back," Clunie cried softly.

"It'll be all right. I promise. One day I'll just set by the pond with my shotgun and kill that old turtle dead. You got my oath on that, Clunie."

Pulling away from his hold on her, she knelt quickly, then handed him a daisy.

II

"RAIN," SIGHED COACH.

Leo Bannon watched Coach Hackman stare out of his office window. Inside, Leo felt grateful for the rain because he didn't feel like practice. "Are we washed out for today, Coach?"

"Yup. The field's a swamp."

Leo smiled inwardly. "Too bad."

"Yeah, 'cause next Tuesday's our opener."

"Guess I'll ship out. See ya, Coach."

"Keep straight."

Central High disgorged its students. Leo searched for Sally Rowe; and saw her, with Macon. Damn her! Who gives a hoot? Not me. No sir, not old Leo Bannon, because what happens in this town is only for now, not forever. I'm not hanging out in this crummy burg for the rest of my life.

The rain had subsided. Yet the new May leaves looked fresher, and greener, the tree trunks blacker than usual.

Leo watched the crowd of kids thin out as the fan of recess dispersed. Home, he thought. They're all trotting home like good little chicks. A bunch of wind-up dolls. Well, I don't feel much like going home. Pa's working nights this week, and he'll be sleeping, so's I can't play the radio. I wish I had a phonograph. The girls said that Sally Rowe got one for Christmas, and a whole stack of records. Probably all that bluegrass crap. Love songs.

Ahead of him, Leo could see Sally with Braddy Macon. Reaching up, he yanked a handful of leaves from a maple, and was instantly rewarded with a shower of raindrops. Hard as he could, he threw back the fistful of leaves at the tree.

"Blow it."

Leo didn't want to go downtown to the soda shop, or anywhere else where he'd have to look at Rowe and Macon. He thought about the book in the school library, the one where the captain of the baseball team gets to take the prettiest gal in the school to the Junior Prom. Big deal. The guy who wrote that stupid book never lived in *this* town.

He felt muggy and hot. If the water in the dam wasn't so cold, he thought, I'd go for a swim. Shed the thread and jump in. Maybe that'd cool me off. Dumb old Coach, always preaching like a priest, telling us the same line of bull that Father Murphy tells us. If you think about girls too much, best you take a cold shower or a cold swim, and you don't get so hot and bothered.

"Hogwash," said Leo.

It don't swing, Father. No way, Coach. There ain't enough icewater at the North Pole to take my mind off Sally Rowe. Or any girl. And what bugs me is that I bet she's hotter than I am. No babe walks the way Sally walks without wanting it. Real bad. She's asking for it, and Macon's too pure or too dumb to give it to her.

"Well, I ain't. Not *me*."

Tonight, I'm taking myself a walk up Maple Avenue, all the way up to where the Rowes live. Soon as it's dark. And I bet I can hide in the bushes, real quiet, and look in Sally's window. Maybe see her skin off her clothes. Yeah, if she knew I was outside, looking in. She'd want to tease some guy until he goes crazy, just looking at her, and not being able to reach up through the window and touch her. She'd peal it off real slow.

"Yeah, that's what she'd do. For sure, if she knew it was Leo Bannon outside looking at her. She'd be pleased as hell to get me all hyped up."

Damn it, I'm up for it right now. Why did it have to rain all day and wash out practice? And there I was, a few minutes back, glad that we'd all get an afternoon to goof off, without old Hackman guffing out orders: Hit to right! Run another lap! Leo, when you're behind the plate, catching, it's okay to drop down on one knee if nobody's on base. But with a runner on first, keep your cleats planted so it'll brace your throw to second. Crap.

"Baseball's for the birds."

Maybe, thought Leo, I'll go down to the pool hall and see if Alfred Patnode is around. Him I can beat. Run the rack and rip off his money. One thing I can do, man, is shoot a mean stick of pool. Guess it's the only thing Pa taught me. Make a firm bridge with your left hand, so the last three fingers tripod it real steady. Thumb under the barrel of the cue and index finger looped over the top so it rests on the tip of your thumb.

Stroke. Always stroke the cue forward with your right hand. Don't punch or poke at the cue ball. Cue high for follow and low for draw. And always play for position on the next shot.

Leo smiled. That's how I beat Alf Patnode, time after time. He's too vacant to ever leave himself a decent lie. All he wants to play is Rotation, so he can slam the yellow 1-ball against all the cushions, and maybe get lucky and sink a big ringer.

Leo saw Clunie. "Pool," he said, "can wait a while."

Yeah, he thought, on account I got better things to do. Clunie Finn. One thing for sure: She'd never be able to squeal on ya; and if she did, who'd believe a word of it?

Yahoo!

Following her, taking his time about catching up, Leo watched her leave town, heading up the dirt road. She was careful, he noticed, not to step in the pools of muddy water that rutted the gravel.

"Nobody on that old road," he said. "Not for near a mile, until you finally come to the Finn place, away out in the boons."

Leo eyed the way Clunie walked, noticing how her body filled out her dress. Damn! he told himself, I gotta be careful. If anybody ever found out about what I got in mind for Clunie Finn, they'd laugh me right out of town. Jail? Yeah, maybe that as well. I could end up in the county slammer.

"Nobody'll find out."

Boy, that Clunie's got a big body. Big and white and warm. She's gonna be like riding on top of a great big pillow. Leo laughed at the thought. A real live pillow that's got legs to roll around on. And she'll be really scared. But she'll be too frightened to yell out. Ha! And before I'm done on her, she won't be thinking of anything but old Leo Bannon, and how much man she's got. More'n she's worth.

"I'll show her."

Clunie was a cinch to follow. In the roadside brush,

moving easily behind tree after tree, Leo kept himself hidden. Even if she turned around, Clunie would never know that he was following her, coming closer by each tree. His body hardened. Mouth open, he felt dry and thirsty. But no hunger was in his throat, or, in his stomach. Farther down, deeper and more agonizing.

Why, he wondered, did I wait so long? I should have done this all year, every damn day after school, until Clunie would wait for me. After today, she'll beg me.

Nearer now, Leo could make out the pattern on the back of Clunie's dress. Butterflies. And I sure like the way that certain butterfly wiggles, he thought. Never did like a skinny gal. With a big body you got more to love, more to hang on to. A big girl's got more strength in her, so's she can fight and kick and bite back.

"No fun if it's easy."

Aloud, Leo said it again, feeling the words come alive. He repeated it. "No fun if it's easy." That's what he'd do! Keep saying it, louder and louder, until he was close to Clunie, and she'd turn around and hear. I can't wait, he thought, to see the look on her stupid face. She'll be afraid of me. Just like the rest of the kids in Central. They're all afraid of Leo Francis Bannon 'cause I got the biggest fists in the school.

"Now what's she up to?"

Stopping at the side of the road, Clunie had bent

over as though to look for something, but Leo couldn't quite see what it was. Her back was to him. It appeared as if she was plucking something.

Flowers? Good, because I'm going to pick her flower, all for myself, and nobody'll know. Except me. Clunie don't count. She's too dumb to know my name or tell anybody about it.

Daisies? Is that what she's collecting? Well, in about one more minute, Clunie Finn is going to forget all about flower picking. All *she's* going to think about is little old Leo and the biggest surprise of her life.

I'm the only man in the school, and this'll prove it. And once I get to Clunie, then I'll take care of Sally Rowe, one of these days. Braddy Macon, too. And perhaps a few others. Let'em all know who's boss.

"I'll show'em all."

Clunie turned around. Leo wanted her to see him; yet for some reason he found himself ducking down to stay out of sight. Am I losing my nerve? he wondered. Am I chicken?

No way. Not old Leo, he thought. To start something means that you've got to finish it, so there's no turning back now. Besides, I want to. I *got to.*

"Clunie!"

Keeping low and hidden, Leo chuckled to himself. I bet she don't know what she heard. Wait'll she sees it's me.

"Clunie! I'm gonna *git* you, girl."

Quickly he ran through the brush, darting past her to a point where he would be between her and her home. Then he slowly straightened up, stepping out of the roadside brush to where Clunie could see him. Walking toward her, he began to slowly unbutton his shirt. No use getting it all tore up.

"Hi there, Clunie. What's that you got in your hand? Daisies?"

Clunie nodded.

"I got a treat for ya, Clunie. A big surprise. And you're really going to love it. Hear?"

"Go away."

Leo shook his head. "Not this time." With an easy gesture, he tossed his shirt over the limb of a sassafras, continuing to walk toward her, hoping she'd notice how tight his jeans were. He smiled.

"You better fight me, Clunie. Even though it won't do no good, baby. Not against a bull like me."

Her face seemed frozen; mouth open, eyes wide, as though a scream had caught inside her throat.

Leo made a grab for her, but she stumbled back, away from him and closer to the roadside. "I'm gonna heft your dress up, baby. You and me are going to have at it. Right now. Right here, where you can kick and scratch. And holler, because ain't nobody gonna hear you. Or help you."

Softly, she said one word, "Braddy."

Leo smiled, catching her hair in his hand, holding

her so she couldn't run farther into the wet brush. "Braddy ain't here. Only me and you, Clunie. But you keep yelling for Braddy all you please."

"Braddy! Help me, Braddy."

"That's it, Clunie. Yell it out. I got you, honey bun. By the hair, and it's going to be now. Now!"

As he tore off her dress, all he heard her say was Macon's name. Over and over. Softly, almost silently.

"Braddy . . . Braddy . . ."

12

"FLORENCE! YOU HOME?"

"Right here in the kitchen, Verna."

In his room, Braddy Macon looked up from *Today's Biology*, listening to the conversation between his mother and their next-door neighbor, Verna Thane.

"You heard the news?"

"No. Radio's been off."

"Gladice Rooking just called up to tell me. It seems that Sheriff Davis found a body. Dead."

"*Who?*"

"Gladice didn't know. All she said was that a child had been killed."

"No! Where?"

"Out on the old county road, just this side of the Finn place. She says the police are out there now. And maybe the county coroner."

"I can't believe it."

"Well, it's true."

"Leastwise," Braddy heard his mother say, "I don't want to believe it. Poor child."

"They took the body to the hospital, dead and all." Verna Thane lowered her voice. "And they said he was . . . half naked."

"Mercy."

"Blood all over him."

His biology book fell to the floor as Braddy Macon ran from his room, out the front door. He saw a man with a supper napkin still tucked in beneath his chin. People were starting their cars, or running next door to tell their neighbors. Everyone was moving, or talking; except for a few of the older folks who only stood on their front porches, hands touching their speechless lips.

Cars were headed up the old road. Braddy hitched a ride for about a mile in Oscar Hillman's old blue Chevy. He then jumped off, dashing into more than a score of people who were already milling around at the roadside. Two uniformed policemen from town were there, next to a squad car beneath its flashing red light, trying to answer a dozen questions and preventing the curious from trampling every clue.

"Please! Please keep back."

Ducking into the underbrush, Braddy worked his

way to where Sheriff Davis and a cop were kneeling. Weeds were beaten flat. In his hand, the policeman held a rust-colored shirt. They talked while Braddy listened.

"We're pretty sure this was the boy's shirt."

"But it ain't tore."

"No. If there'd been a struggle—"

"It'd got ripped."

Leo's! Braddy's breath caught. It was Leo Bannon's shirt, the one he so often wore to school. Dirty or clean. Braddy's mouth was open as he tried to gasp air.

Leo Bannon dead?

Bending over, the policeman lifted up several wilted flowers.

"Daisies."

"Yeah. Must've been picking daisies beside the roadway. Here's more."

"We gotta get the guy that done this."

"Don't worry. We'll catch him."

Braddy waited, hidden and listening, looking through the leaves at the wilted bouquet of daisies. Darn you, Clunie! But it couldn't be Clunie's fault, he thought. It just had to be Leo's, because Bannon started trouble with everybody. And he'd picked on Clunie before. Plenty of times.

What'll I do?

Braddy covered his face with both hands. Body trembling, he tried to think. Opening his eyes, he stared again at the daisies that still drooped lifelessly from the cop's big hand.

Should I tell?

Best I don't, he thought, because I'm not certain. Just guessing. Sure, it's Leo's shirt. Or maybe it is. Yet is that proof that Leo's the victim? Or is Leo still alive because he attacked someone else?

Braddy's eyes felt hot and moist.

I can't hide here all evening. Mama will wonder where I ran off to. And why I just scooted out of the house at suppertime.

"Yeah," Braddy heard Sheriff Davis say, "we gotta act fast."

"You got the roads blocked?"

Sheriff Davis nodded. "We got a car uproad about a mile, and the town police sealed off the state road and the lake road, east of here."

"Was he on foot?"

"Who knows?"

"Maybe he cut cross-meadow."

"Possible. Even a chance he lit out for the swamp."

"You know, once he saw what he done, maybe he just hightailed it away from the roadside, off yonder."

"Any word from the hospital?"

"Nope."

"Found anything?"

"Precious little. A handful of dead daisies and the poor lad's shirt."

"Got any suspicions?"

"Nary a one. Oh, there's the troublesome element in this town. You know, the usual window-smashers, and we get our share of Saturday night fists. A wild bunch across the railroad that runs back of the paper mill."

"Think it's one of them?"

"Honest, I don't know what to think."

"You sent for anybody?"

"Like who?"

"Detectives."

"Yeah, I already got one on the car radio. He's up in Dudley checking on a break-in they had last night at a gas station. He'll come pronto."

"Who's coming?"

"Charlie Cross, and he's the best in the county, or so they say."

"He'll be madder than Bedlam when he gets here and sees every shoe in town tromping all over the evidence. I give orders to Herb, you know, to tell folks to keep their distance."

"Yeah, but you know people."

"Curious as cats. Every dang one of 'em thinks he's Sherlock Holmes."

"It's going to be hairy when we catch the guy."

"Reckon so. Some dang fool will bring a rope and try to save the taxpayers the price of a trial. And I'd be tempted to turn my back and let 'em do it."

Braddy Macon's legs began to cramp. Yet he could not force himself to move. Seems as though I ought to do something, he thought. But what? Should I go to see Clunie, or maybe just go back home? Mama will be waiting supper. The thought of eating caused his stomach to heave. He wanted to throw up.

"Right here. This is the spot." Sheriff Davis pointed at the ground.

"Doc Hall's at the hospital. We figure the body was discovered soon after the killing, and maybe Doc can pinpoint the exact time."

"He'll write up a report."

"Yeah."

"Trouble is, reports don't help a whale of a lot. That's what Charlie Cross says. He claims that the best place to start is with the next of kin."

"For the killer?"

"That's what he told me. Charlie says that folks usual get murdered by a member of their family. Somebody close."

"People do creepy things."

"Sure enough do."

Angry voices were heard from near the road, causing both men to turn and listen. Braddy watched them move away to investigate. Creeping forward, Braddy Macon saw the fallen weeds, trampled flat from a death struggle. And one more wilted daisy, its stem twisted and bent, lying very still.

The irate voice beyond the trees became a shout, causing Braddy to scurry, finding a closer hiding place in order to hear what was happening.

"My daughter!"

Braddy heard the voice of Patrick Finn.

"Clunie didn't come home after school. I heard there's trouble down here. Sol Ikin told me. So I come. He said there's been a killing. Where's my daughter?"

"Easy now, Pat."

"She's missing. *Clunie!*" He yelled her name several times. "Where is she? Where?"

"Please don't go in there, Mr. Finn."

"No! I gotta find my Clunie."

"Patrick, it wasn't her. It was another child that got killed."

"Clunie!"

"Please . . . please, Mr. Finn, you can't go in there until the detectives get here. Sheriff's orders."

"*Clunie!*"

"It was a boy, Pat. Not a girl."

"No! You're all liars. Clunie didn't come home. She's gone. Somebody hurt Clunie. I feel it. I know, I know . . ."

The man was weeping, hollering his rage.

"I know Clunie's dead."

13

"PAPA!"

The sun hung lower in the sky, half hidden by the tops of the trees. Clunie Finn shivered at the oncoming darkness, for she was seldom allowed outside the house after supper. But, being afraid to go home, she had eaten no evening meal.

Maybe, she worried, Papa will come and find me. He'll be mad. Sometimes he talks loud and throws the frypan in the kitchen when I do bad things. Like wander off to chase the chipmunks that live in the stone fence beyond our orchard. Closing her eyes, she could see her father's face growing red, and his hands becoming fists. Yet, she thought, Papa don't spank me no more. Or hurt me. But I know he's angry right now.

Papa's not mean. Leo is.

Why did I hurt Leo? I don't want to hurt anyone. But Leo was tearing my dress and clawing at me. So I had to make Leo stop. I spank Leo with that hunk of wood I pick up, so he won't do bad things to me anymore.

After that, I hit all his clothes.

"I'm sorry, Leo."

The prickers inside the juniper bushes where she was hiding began to stab into her arms whenever Clunie tried to move. The juniper was bad, like Leo. But sometimes, in the summertime when there wasn't any school, the little blue berries tasted cool to chew on. The berries weren't mean. They were sweet, like all the baby ducklings.

And like Braddy.

Why couldn't Leo be like Braddy instead of like Leo all the time? she thought. I hope Leo gets better. Papa say I'm a strong girl, and now Leo will know how hard I can hit and leave me alone. If he gets up. Tonight I'll say him in my prayers.

"God bless Leo."

Speaking his name was like standing at the edge of the duck pond, calling for the mother duck to come back. But she never does, because that ugly old snapper pulled her under, into the mud. Leo's not a turkey. Not even if Braddy say so. No, Leo is a snapper turtle, because he wants to do ugly things, like pull people down and hit and hurt. And make me cry.

Just remembering, Clunie was almost crying.

"I didn't mean it, Leo. All I wanted was to walk home from school, like Papa say to do, and bring him daisies."

Best I don't go home.

I can't tell Papa. I don't want to hurt him the way I hurt Leo. And Papa will look hurted if'n he find out what I did beside the road. Then I ran away. Kids are bad to run away from home, Papa say.

Where can I go?

"Papa, please sew up my dress."

My clothes are all tore. All tore to bits. I just wanted to pick daisies. It's May. I want to be pretty, like May. And like Braddy. I don't want to be ugly like Leo, all bloody and still.

"Leo and the mother duck aren't ever going to come back. And I'm shameful. It's my fault."

As she stood up, Clunie's legs were still shaking. Maybe, she thought, because Leo had been talking to her about her legs, and saying all those strange things. She slowly stepped out of the clump of juniper, her hands holding the tatters of her dress.

Walking down the hill, she could hear the water, a rushing sound that grew louder as she walked closer to the pond above the dam. Her hands felt so sticky and stained.

Clunie tried to rub off the blood. "I want to wash my hands."

There was a wall around the dam. It was not very high, yet high enough to prevent Clunie from reaching her hand down to the water. Maybe, she thought, if I lie down on my belly, I can reach the water with my fingers. Then I can wash my hands clean. I don't like to be dirty. Not nice. Leo is dirty. Her throat tightened as her nose remembered how Leo smelled. Sour, and hot. Today he had attacked her in a different way.

"I was very mean, too. And I sorry."

Lying flat, atop the uneven wall where some stones had broken loose, Clunie stretched down her hand. The water felt cold. The pond looked so very dark, almost black. In the daytime, fishing here with Papa, the water was silvery, sort of like the pretty sides of the shiner fish they caught on their bamboo poles.

Not now. The pond looked inky and lifeless.

"Here, fishy fishies."

I wonder if the shiners will swim up and nibble on my fingers, she thought, like they think I got worms. No, I best not think about the fish. I have to wash off my sticky hands. And the front of my dress. Papa like to keep stuff clean. So does Teacher. Clean milk pails and a clean blackboard. Cal won't help wash off the board, but I always help.

"Teacher say I'm a good helper."

I like to turn the blackboard blacker, like when you

put the wet sponge on it. It wash black as night. Then the good part comes. I get to watch the blackboard dry off, real slow, and the blacky streaks get up thinner and shorter until the board is gray again. Clean as a whistle, Teacher say.

I like school.

But I hated the day when Cal push me into the closet and shutted the door. I remember. It was dark inside. I screamed for Teacher, and Papa, to come and fetch me out. Cal not nice sometimes.

Papa say if I do bad things, people could come to our house and take me off. They lock me up. Not in a jailhouse. But Papa say the hospital for people like me is sort of like a jail, and he don't want me to have to go there. He cry when he say it. Then he wipe his tears on his shirt and hug me very hard, like a promise.

Papa don't like the law.

He say the law can come and take people away and lock them up, just like we shut up the chickens. So they don't get harm, or hurt people. Papa say I won't get shutted up as long as I stay good, and obey.

"Papa, I'm not good anymore."

I hit Leo.

Pulling up dripping handfuls of water from the pond, Clunie bathed her hands, washing her neck, and feeling the coolness freshen her face. May is too early to go in wading, her father had told her. Besides, this pond above the dam was big, not little like the duckpond. The water here was dark and deep. Clunie cautioned herself to be careful and not fall in.

"I can't swim."

Papa know how. He know all kinds of stuff, like the way to plant corn, and dig up potatoes, and *can*. We put by for winter, Clunie remembered Mrs. Jennings come, and she let me help do the canning every August. We boil the turnips and fill up the jars. And put the jars in water and simmer out the air so the turnips don't foul.

"Mrs. Jennings."

Sometimes it help to say things out loud, like names. And it make me feel I not so all alone. In the closet, I was alone in the dark, yelling out names. But I didn't holler for Mrs. Jennings because I wasn't hungry.

"I'm hungry now."

Clunie thought about the turnips, in a bowl, all sparkled on top with brown sugar. In the spring they would make maple sugar—boil down the sap to render it sweet. And thick. For pancakes and turnips. It would make your mouth sticky.

Clunie remembered the blood. Even though my hands are clean and wet, I still feel Leo's blood. Sticky, like maple sap. I like to drink sap right out of the tap spout because it's so sweet. Sort of like Papa and Teacher and Mrs. Jennings.

And like Braddy.

Clunie splashed more water on the front of her dress. I don't want to feel dirty anymore, she thought. Not dirty and not mean. I was really bad at Leo because he was going to be bad at me.

"I'm strong, Leo."

Stronger than you are. Papa and I are farmers. Grandpa was a farmer, too. Right on our land. And when I help do the haying, with Papa, we get to eat all we want because of the hard work. But the seeds itch my neck. They blow off the hay wagon and sneak down the back of my dress and glue to all my sweat.

I wish it was haying time now. I could eat a big meal and not get fat. Cal ought to eat more. He's skinny. And his eyes can look at you and he don't see nothing. Just air. He can't count. I can count. Teacher say it's good to count up things. If the cake we bake calls for six eggs, it don't pan out so hot if'n we mere stir in three.

Teacher know.

I love her so much. She know everything. Even before I act sorry.

Clunie wondered if her teacher would know about what she had done to poor Leo. Just what the snapper turtle did to the mother duck. No!

"Help me, please. Somebody."

I can't get my dress clean. But I'm not going to take

it off and wash it. How can I do it? Maybe if I jump in the water my dress'll rinse clean. Then Papa won't see the blood.

Clunie leaned down once more, shifting her weight atop the retaining wall, unsettling a loose rock. The wall gave beneath her, crumbling, the rough bits of old mortar suddenly failing. Fragments splashed into the pond. Her hands fought to hold, but her weight pulled her over.

Clunie fell into cold darkness.

14 🌿

"CLUNIE!"

Braddy Macon ran. Ahead of him, beyond the pasture and above the peaks of the pines, a soft pink serpent of sunset lay along the distant hills.

"Clunie Finn, where are you?"

Repeatedly, he called her name—lungs aching, legs hurting from the long run. Yet he wouldn't quit until he found her. No use looking at the Finn farm. But she wouldn't be far away. Her urge to run home, he thought, following the trouble with Leo, would be too compelling.

Maybe I should double back into town and round up some of the kids. Wick would help. And so would Sally, and Helen, and the guys on the baseball team.

Maybe even Alfred Patnode.

"Clunie!"

Where would she go? What does she like besides crayons and daisies and . . . *ducks?*

Sitting on a rock, just to catch his breath, Braddy whipped his neck in a wide arc, staring at the row of shrub willows that divided the meadow from the crickbed. Water? Just maybe Clunie would be thirsty. Had she run until her mouth was dry, as his was now?

Straining to his feet, Braddy hurried toward the stream, thrashing through the thick underbrush. Thorns cut his face, slashing into his cheek and brow until he stopped, panting heavily while his fingers gently removed the long, dry curving cane of blackberry.

"Damn it." Prickers stung his hands.

Shoes and all, Braddy splashed into the shallow water. Upstream? Downstream? Had she come this way; and if so, which direction? Listening, he heard only the soft ripple of the crick water and a choir of evening insects, humming in the deepening darkness.

The light was fast fading. No Clunie. Maybe she was really lost. Scared and shaking, too frightened even to head for home or confront her father.

Braddy saw it!

Less than twenty feet from where he stood slapping a mosquito, he spotted a wisp of cloth that hung from the tip of a bramble. Splashing silver drops as he leaped over the round crickbed stones, Braddy ran to the cloth. Snatching it, he felt its much-washed

softness. Clunie's dress? It sort of had to be hers.
Squinting at the fabric, he thought he saw part of a
pale yellow butterfly, in the print of the cloth.

Yes. It was hers.

"Clunie!"

No echo. As if her name was absorbed and
deadened by the brushy banks. Yelling again, his voice
sounded lifeless, his fingers gripping the cloth inside
his clenched fist.

"Roast in hell, Bannon!" Braddy yelled up at the
sky. "Can you hear me, Leo? Listen, you rotten
stinker. You got what you deserved, didn't you
Bannon?"

In a rage, Braddy Macon threw the torn hunk of
cloth into the crick, watching it float away. I'm a fool,
he thought, standing here in the water wasting time
cussing out Leo.

"Where are you, Clunie?"

And then, a few feet beyond where he had torn the
cloth from the bramble, he noticed the bent trunks of
small trees. Saplings, less than knee high, several of
them. Leaping forward, Braddy scrambled up the
bank, leaving the crick but finding it again as its elbow
curved around to corner him in its crook.

All he could see was the memory of the torn rag
from Clunie's dress, floating away. Downstream! Yes,
as if the scrap of cloth with its little butterfly had been
trying to inform him, to show him which way to

pursue. There was only one place where Clunie would be in danger.

Above the dam.

Ignoring the torture in his legs, he ran; faster now, because he knew where he was headed. Ever since he could recall Mama had warned him about the dam, the one place that always seemed to attract children. Just a year ago, one of the Willingson kids had strayed off. And they'd found her broken body, washed into the cattails facedown, white and dead. Below the falls.

"Clunie!"

As he ran, the sound of the waterfall swelled in his ears, as if washing away his hollering of Clunie's name. Louder and louder. Yet it was a distant sound which failed to smother a noise he heard that was closer. Nearer. A weak splashing.

"Help me."

The words, the voice, pierced him as he gained the wall, his sloshing shoes running along its rim. And then he saw Clunie beating at the water with her heavy arms, drifting slowly toward the lip of the dam.

The shock of the cold water seemed to stop his heart, but he swam toward her, gasping for breath. Black water stung his nose, and he felt the weight of it suck at his shoes. The current was stronger than he had imagined. May, people said—May and June were dangerous times to try to swim the pond because of the melting mountain snow and all the April rain. Add to that the rain today. That hard, beating, driving rainstorm he'd seen from inside the school windows. All day long until about three o'clock.

"Hang on, Clunie."

A mouthful of water replaced his yell, burning his lungs. Braddy coughed, choking, as his leaden legs fought to kick him forward. Ahead of him, Clunie's white hands clawed at a dark and mossy wall. Her head sunk.

Braddy reached her. "Clunie . . . Clunie . . ."

The jolt of her arms around his neck supplied more force than he could handle, dunking his face beneath the surface, as he screamed her name into nothing but bubbles. No air. Her weight was against him, strong and cold and holding him down so that he could no longer breathe. Air! Please, please, I want air. His water-deaf ears heard the muffled drumbeats of their struggling, while Clunie tried to climb his body.

"No . . . Clunie, no . . ."

Could she hear him? How? He could no longer hear himself. Clunie's weight held him under, until he lifted his feet far enough to brace against her gut, to push her away, while his hands were still clawing at the water. The fingers of his right hand slid down the slime of the wall. Why was the wall moving? The current was sucking at them, faster now, even though he tried to fight it. The flow was even stronger than Clunie.

A wire?

Somehow his fingers closed on it, holding on, feeling the rusted metal cut into his right hand. Using his left, he grabbed Clunie's hair. Yanking her, he saw her white shoulder rise above the surface. Jerking and twisting, he managed to force her face upward to allow her to breathe.

Beside him, her white body thrashed beneath the black water, her hands clutching at his face. One of her fingers stabbed into his eye and he was sick with pain. Yet his grip on her hair, and the wire, held.

"Clunie, don't be scared. It's me, Braddy."

"Braddy—" she gasped at him. "Braddy."

"Yeah, I'm here. You're okay. Long as I can hang on. But don't fight me, Clunie. No! No, please don't. Please."

"Braddy?"

"Yes, yes—but don't pull me under, or I can't— hold on. We'll both drown."

"Help me. Help."

"Okay. Okay now, Clunie. You don't have to be frightened."

"Leo—"

"Leo's dead."

"They—the people come and lock me away—"

"You didn't mean to do it."

Braddy tried to talk, but again his mouth flooded, choking his words.

"You'll be fine, Clunie."

"They come, like Papa say. And they take me off to shut me up. Like the chickens."

Again her arms strangled his neck, forcing his face under, where he could neither hear nor speak. Air!

"—and they shut me up because I hurt Leo."

"No Clunie, no. Leo was going to hurt you."

"Don't lock me away."

Braddy's lungs fought for air while his mind struggled for reason. If only, he thought, I could breathe. For some reason, the cruel chant started to sing in his ears:

Clunie Finn, Clunie Finn . . . Lock her up in a loony bin.

Over and over, he heard their teasing.

"I love Braddy."

Her words stung him, reaching inside him to rip at his bowels, more painful than the wire that wanted to cut through his fingers.

"I can't hold on, Clunie."

"Braddy—don't let 'em—"

"I won't, Clunie. No, I won't let them lock you up."

As he spoke, he knew they would.

"Stop it, Clunie. You're drowning me. We'll both go under." Braddy coughed, as the heat of near death burned his lungs. The wire? God, he thought, I can't feel the wire. My hand's got such a cramp I can't feel it. My arm's coming out of my shoulder.

I want to let go.

"Let loose of my hair. Please." Clunie said.

"No."

"Let go, Braddy. You hear?"

"Clunie, don't be scared."

"Braddy, do daisies grow in Heaven?"

Her words closed his eyes. He was sobbing, feeling his stomach convulse in grief, knowing he couldn't hold onto a wire that he could no longer feel bite his icy hand.

"Yes, Clunie, daisies grow in Heaven. All the time. Because up in Heaven it's always May."

She was kissing his face. It was all he could feel, only her cold lips lightly against his wet cheek. No, nobody will lock her up. She'll always be free.

"Good-bye, Braddy."

She was too strong for him, fighting his grip, ripping at his hand. As his stiffening fingers released their hold on her hair, he watched her face slip away from him. Clunie wasn't struggling anymore.

She was smiling.

ROBERT NEWTON PECK comes from a long line of Vermont farmers. His first novel, *A Day No Pigs Would Die* tells of a Vermont boyhood on a family farm, and many of his books for younger readers are rooted in his own experience. Among these are the popular stories about Soup: *Soup, Soup and Me,* and *Soup For President,* which vividly portray the adventures of Peck's childhood. He has also written several historical novels, including a trilogy about Fort Ticonderoga—*Fawn, Hang for Treason,* and *The King's Iron*—and the recently published *Eagle Fur.* He now lives in Longwood, Florida where he serves each February as the director of Rollins College Writers Conference. He also sings in a barbershop quartet, plays ragtime piano, and is an enthusiastic speaker. His hobby is visiting schools "to turn kids on to books."